Stranger in Thunder Basin

Books by John D. Nesbitt

For the Norden Boys
Lonesome Range
Black Hat Butte
Red Wind Crossing
Rancho Alegre
Raven Springs
Coyote Trail
Black Diamond Rendezvous
Man from Wolf River
Not a Rustler
West of Rock River
North of Cheyenne
Poacher's Moon
Adventures of the Ramrod Rider
A Good Man to Have in Camp
Keep the Wind in Your Face
Shadows on the Plain
Field Work
Blue Horse Mesa: Western Stories
Antelope Sky: Stories of the Modern West
Seasons in the Fields: Stories of a Golden West
Blue Is Not the Word / Buckskin Trail
Rose of Greenwood
Gather My Horses
Trouble at the Redstone
Death at Dark Water
Stranger in Thunder Basin

Two Novellas:
Dead for the Last Time
Trouble in the Labor Camp

For more information
visit: www.SpeakingVolumes.us

Stranger in Thunder Basin

John D. Nesbitt

SPEAKING VOLUMES, LLC
NAPLES, FLORIDA
2025

Stranger in Thunder Basin

Copyright © 2009 by John D. Nesbitt

All rights reserved. No part of this book may be reproduced or transmitted in any form or by any means without written permission.

ISBN 979-8-89022-313-5

for Dave McCabe

Chapter One

From the beginning there rose a memory ancient as blood.

The long, cold wind had quit blowing, but the sun was still shut out. Under a grey sky, the dunes of snow lay hard-packed—domed and smooth on the windward side, ridged and sculpted on the leeward. The boy could walk up on top of a drift and, it seemed to him, stand in the sky. When Pa-Pa stood on the next drift over, he looked taller than ever.

All morning, Pa-Pa dug walkways from the cabin, first to the outhouse and then to the barn. Pa-Pa worked with a steady motion, carving out snow and tossing it to one side or the other. Orly the dog watched, looked up at Eddie. Pa-Pa was quiet, no sound but the slice of the shovel and the thump of the snow when it landed. At one point on the way to the barn, the passageway was higher than Eddie's cap.

Pa-Pa worked on. When he cleared the door of the barn, Eddie and the dog followed him inside. The air was as thin and cold as outside. The horses whoofed and snuffled. Pa-Pa gave them grain from a burlap sack, hard pale sliding seeds that he called oats.

Pa-Pa carried the round-headed shovel and the square one. Eddie walked beside him, and Orly trotted ahead. A big drift lay across the road. Pa-Pa said he was going to have to clear it out before they could go anywhere. He started digging, first with the square shovel and then with the round one. He began on the right and worked across, then went to his right again and cut deeper into the drift, carving out slabs of solid white cake. As loose snow gathered at his feet, he scooped it up and tossed it as well.

Now with his shovel he held a big square piece in front of Eddie's eyes. It was cleaner than lard, cleaner than the whitest ice cream. Then he tossed it, and it fell apart when it landed.

"I'm sure you're wondering why I throw it all to the right side here."

Eddie looked at him without saying anything.

"Well, I don't want the wind to blow it back in. If I throw it to the left and a big wind comes, all the loose and crumbly stuff'll fill in, and I'll have to come back tomorrow and do the same thing."

He stabbed the shovel in the snowbank and took a deep breath, then opened and closed his hands. The creased leather gloves looked like part of him, as did the canvas coat and the sweat-lined hat. Pa-Pa, solid and tall against a grey sky, his weathered face like deerhide, his silvery hair flowing to cover his ears and touch his collar. He took another breath and went back to work.

Eddie rolled in the loose snow, tumbling with Orly and teasing him. Above, the grey sky went everywhere, and Eddie could not tell where the sky ended and the world began. Here below, his coat was a dull black, and his mittens, itchy as the coat, were dark grey. Orly was black and white, but the white was almost yellow compared with the snow.

"Here," came Pa-Pa's voice. "Stand up. You're gettin' too much snow on you."

Eddie felt himself being pulled up in the scratchy coat. Pa-Pa took off the stocking cap, shook it out, then pressed it back over Eddie's ears. With his leather gloves he brushed the dry snow off of the boy's coat, turning him one way and the other. Eddie felt snow melting on the back of his neck, then a relaxing of the coat.

"I wonder who this is." Pa-Pa's hands let go.

Across the top of the snowdrift, Eddie could see a man on a horse—a dark, narrow shape against the bleak background. Pa-Pa held the shovel at rest and watched the rider come closer. Sound carried as the horse's hooves rose from the snow and punched in again.

The stranger came to a stop on the other side of the drift. Both horse and rider loomed dark. Wisps of steam floated from the animal's nose and mouth. The horse's body carried a dull color between black and dark brown. A lighter brown showed along the edges of the nose, the forehead, and the ears, while the mane and tail ran to pure black. The rider wore a flat-brimmed, flat-crowned black hat, dull with old dust. He had a narrow face with a long, thin nose, a pair of beady, close-set eyes, and thin lips. The lower part of his face, tapered, lay in shadow-like stubble, and a dark neckerchief covered his throat. He wore a scratchy-looking coat the color of a burned-out fire log.

Pa-Pa's voice came out in the cold air. "What can I do for you?"

The thin lips moved. "I'm lookin' for Jake Bishop."

"That's me."

The stranger cast his beady glance at Eddie, then back at Pa-Pa. "Need to talk to you. Just you and me."

"The kid's no harm."

"Little pitchers have big ears."

"I said he's no harm. Tell me what's on your mind."

The stranger came off his horse, slow and stiff-life. When he turned around, he had his coat unbuttoned and his gloves in his left hand. "I've got a message. Not for the ears of little boys." With his right hand he touched the hem of his coat.

Pa-Pa turned to look at Eddie. "Here, Sonny," he said, reaching into his coat pocket and bringing out a piece of pale, hard candy. "Take this, and go get me the hatchet I use to split kindling."

Eddie looked up into his face and saw nothing to understand.

"Here, take it, and go get me the hatchet."

Eddie put the candy into his mouth, tasting the peppermint as he knew he would.

"Go, now. Take the dog." Pa-Pa turned him around and gave him a push.

Eddie followed the footprints they had made coming out from the cabin. Even Pa-Pa's tracks had not sunk in very deep, the snow was so hard. Orly pranced along, leaving no tracks at all. The cabin was getting closer.

A loud, cracking sound came from behind and made him jump. It was a gunshot, just like Pa-Pa made.

Orly had broken into a run and now stopped to turn around. Eddie was frozen, half-pivoting, not sure whether to run to the cabin or look back. Everything was quiet now. He knew it had been the sound of a gun, but Pa-Pa wasn't wearing his, not when he worked with a shovel.

Eddie turned. The dark stranger was climbing onto his horse, then reining it around and riding away with flecks of snow kicking up. Where was Pa-Pa?

Eddie ran forward until the bottom of the snowdrift came into view. He saw Pa-Pa lying where he had shoveled out the snow. Eddie stopped. His heart was beating stronger than he had ever known, and a cold, prickly feeling ran through his scalp, face, neck, and shoulders.

He walked forward. He had a strange sensation, one he had never felt before. Something big had happened, like a crack in the sky or the edge of the earth falling off. But the sky was still there, grey stretching out forever, and so was the earth, white in every direction with a dark speck in the distance.

Closer now, he saw Pa-Pa lying in the snow where he had dug and trampled. The dun-colored hat had fallen a few feet away, and his full head of silvery hair lay still against the white snow. His eyes were closed, and his weathered face had relaxed. His right hand lay across his chest, while his left, also gloved, seemed to reach for the shovel that had fallen beside him.

All the world was still, and Pa-Pa stillest of all. Then Eddie saw a stain of red seeping through the canvas coat where it touched the snow and stained the crystals. He felt tears come to his eyes as his throat swelled up.

He tried to swallow, and he realized the candy was still in his mouth. He took a deep breath and tried to hold himself from getting dizzy. Then he let go, and the tears fell. With the dog at his side, also silent, Eddie looked at this person who was so familiar to him. He knew Pa-Pa would not finish digging out the snow, or have to come back tomorrow, or ever speak, or build a fire, or saddle a horse again. Nothing would be the same.

Eddie looked off into the cold distance. The speck had disappeared, but the boy knew it had all happened for real. A man had come and done this, a man who looked like a coiled black bullwhip. Eddie thought hard and brought up a picture of the man as he stepped down from his horse and turned around. The face came to him now—a shadowy face with close-set eyes, thin nose and lips, and a narrow chin. He would know that face if he ever saw it again.

Chapter Two

Ed felt the heat of the glowing coals as he stepped toward the forge. He could feel it through the leather gauntlets and apron, but he knew the real heat, dry and searing, when it spread across his face. Wincing, he stuck the tongs into the red-orange center, plucked out the strap of metal, and took it to the anvil. With his hand sledge, he pounded and pounded until the metal looked flat. Still holding the tongs, he lifted the piece and turned it, sighted along the edge, and thought it looked all right except for a small lift at the end. He turned the piece over, set it on the anvil, and pounded it again. Then he stepped back, leaving it to cool on its own.

Metal was always coming in bent and needed to be straightened. Strap hinges like this one, wagon braces, rods, pry bars, channel iron, angle iron, flat iron. Emerson kept the lighter work for himself—branding irons, fireplace pokers, roasting spits, grill work. It seemed as if he didn't want Ed to know how to do anything but the most common work. When he turned out something like a poker or a meat hook, he gave it to Ed to put a point on it. Ed would take his place at the grindstone, work the treadle, and watch the sparks fly.

All winter long, whenever the day-to-day jobs were caught up, Ed sharpened blades from mowing machines and threshers. In winter the door was closed, holding in the smell of hot, smoky metal along with the warmth. Even with the door closed, the thump of the treadle and the screech of iron on coarse stone did not shut out the stamp and boom of the steam-powered rock crusher two blocks down, that ran twelve hours a day, six days out of seven.

Now the door was open. The sun was moving back north, and most of the snow had melted. Ed could look out through the doorway and see some of the life of the town, such as it was. Today he kept an eye out, wondering if he would see the girl again, but he did not stray from his work. He went back to the forge, pumped the bellows, and stuck in the second hinge.

When time for noon dinner came, Emerson hit the triangle. It was something he took pleasure in, not only to let the help know they had permission to stop and eat but to bring out a heavy ringing sound from a piece of equipment he was proud of. It was a large, thick triangle, a foot long on each side, made from an old crowbar. It hung on a chain from a rafter. Whenever someone new came into the shop and remarked about it, Emerson liked to tell its story. A man who had worked for him several years back had traveled through the hardrock mining country in the high Sierra, in California. He had seen a triangle like this at the mouth of a mine, and one day when he came across a crowbar long enough, he made a triangle just like it. He left it as a gift to Emerson. Whenever Ed looked at it, he was impressed by the neatness of the work, the evenness of the angles, and he wondered at the heat and force it would take to bend that bar until the flanged tip came around to rest within an inch of the crook. There seemed to be mystery to it as well, with the claw of the crook pointing like an ancient symbol into the empty space of the triangle.

Ed took dinner at the boarding house as always, eating yesterday's bread and today's hot stew. He did not see the girl, though she had said the evening before that she was staying two days. Among the boarders the talk ran to weather, a plague of grasshoppers in Kansas, a big ditch project farther south, and a man from Nebraska who was wanted for embezzlement. Ed finished his dinner and went out to loaf on the front porch, where the chug of the rock crusher carried on the air.

About an hour into the afternoon, Emerson finished shoeing a coach horse and told Ed to lead it out for him. It was a large chestnut gelding, sleek with good feed and glossy in the spring afternoon. Emerson stood in the shade of the doorway and watched the horse's feet as Ed walked the animal out into the street, around in a semicircle, and back to the shop door.

"Take him around again," said Emerson, with his chin lifted.

Ed took another turn, his hand on the lead rope under the horse's chin, his leather apron rumpling as he marched, bareheaded, in the sunlight. Just before he turned toward the shop, he saw the girl. He waved, and she waved back. Then he led the horse to Emerson, who nodded.

* * * * *

The girl came to supper after most of the boarders had eaten. She was with the same woman as the night before, a middle-aged woman who spoke little and looked like business. Mrs. Willis, who ran the boarding house, called them "ladies," but it was evident that she and the other woman knew each other as equals who cooked, washed, and scrubbed. The women had the same plain appearance, with no jewelry or face powder or lipstick, no bangles or shawls or bright colors. If Mrs. Willis had sat down and the woman had stood up to ladle the soup, Ed would not have been surprised.

The girl, on the other hand, was a fresher flower. From where he sat ten feet away, Ed admired her dark hair and eyes and her red lips. She wore a plain smock of bluish grey, but it did not conceal the pert bosom of a young woman. Even if she was going to stay but one night more, he yearned to know her.

He dawdled with the last of his potatoes, took time to drink his coffee, until he and the two females were the last ones at the table. Mrs. Willis had cleared the other plates, so he moved down to an empty place across from the girl. The woman, who was sitting on the girl's left, cast him a sideways glance but kept to herself.

"Excuse me," he said, looking straight at the girl, "I don't mean to be forward, but I sat across from you last night. You might remember. We talked a little."

A pleasant expression flickered as she gave a light smile and said, "Oh, yes."

"You said you were going to be here just one more night."

"That's right."

"Well, I thought it would be—just terrible—if I didn't get to say hello again."

Her dark eyes settled on him. "That's nice of you."

"Of course, I don't even know your name."

She smiled and gave a shake of the head. "And I don't know yours."

"Oh. It's Edward. Edward Dawes."

"I see. Are you from here in Glenrose?"

"Right now. But not originally." Silence hung, so he spoke again. "I grew up in Silver Springs, down south from here, for the first few years at least. I lived with my, um, grandfather, and then he—died." This was always the hard part. He had not yet found a smooth way to get through it.

She frowned. "I'm sorry to hear that."

He shrugged and said, "Well, it can't be changed."

"And your parents?"

"I don't know them." Now it was easier. "I was adopted by a man named Dawes, and like a lot of people, he took me in so he could get free work out of me. He had a farm down on the Platte, not too far from Nebraska, so I grew up doin' all that kind of work. But when I got old enough, I came here. I work in the blacksmith shop, you know."

"I thought that was you."

He let out a breath. He felt relaxed now. "I don't mean to talk so much, but you asked."

"Oh, you barely said anything."

"Well, in a way there's not much to tell. But in others, there's a lot. You know." Ed felt a glow of warmth in his face.

"Oh, yes."

Ed cast a glance at the older woman, who was buttering a slice of bread and acting as if she hadn't heard a word. From the first moment the night before, he had assumed the woman was not this girl's mother, but he didn't know where to begin asking the girl about herself. Feeling clumsy, he said, "How about yourself? I mean, if I never got to see you again, at least I'd like to know your name."

"It's Ravenna," she said. "Ravenna Owens."

"That's a pretty name."

"Thank you."

He waited, but she didn't say anything more. He felt that time was slipping away, so he took a stab. "Which way are you traveling?" he asked.

"West."

"Oh, I see." After a pause, he added, "Do you like it here?"

"I don't know yet." She touched her napkin to her lips. "You see, I'm not from here."

"Oh."

"I'm like you." She let her dark eyes meet his. "I'm an orphan, too. I was adopted out of an orphanage in Lincoln, by a family that had a farm down by Crete. That's in Nebraska, too."

"I've heard of it."

"They did the same thing. They wanted someone to milk cows and churn butter, wash clothes and do the housework. But Mr. Gregory wasn't very nice, so I ran away and went back to the orphanage. Then

I went to work for Mrs. Porter's sister—this is Mrs. Porter—working in a café."

The woman at Ravenna's left smiled and nodded.

Ed did the same and said, "Pleased to meet you."

"But Mr. Gregory found out where I was, and kept coming around, so we decided it would be best for me to move. I took the train out here to go to work for Mrs. Porter."

"I hope it turns out well for you."

"So do I."

He hesitated, not wanting to be put in the same category as Mr. Gregory. On the other hand, he doubted that Mrs. Porter would try to keep her business place a secret. "Well," he said, "if I'm ever in your town, it would be a—" he fumbled until he found the words—"an honor to pay my respects."

Ravenna turned to Mrs. Porter. "It's Litch, isn't it?"

"Yes," said the woman. "My place is called the Iris. It's by far the best boarding house in that town."

"I'm sure it is. Whenever I get to Litch, and who knows when that'll be, I'll know what to look for."

* * * * *

Ed was grinding points on the feet of a campfire tripod when Jory Stoner came into the shop. Jory was a happy-go-lucky young cowboy who came into town about once a month. He was lean and not very tall, clean-shaven, with brown hair and brown eyes topped off with a wide-brimmed hat. At the moment he carried a pair of hobbles in his left hand, and as usual he was smiling.

"Got a little job," he said.

Ed set the tripod free-standing on the packed floor. "What's that?"

Jory held the hobbles apart, one in each hand, to show that they were separated. One had a D-ring attached, and the other had a D-ring plus about five inches of chain. "Need to hook these together."

"How'd they come apart?"

"Don't know. That's how I got 'em."

Emerson appeared on Jory's left. Raising his chin and looking down his nose, he said, "Go ahead and forge a link for him." He turned away and left the two young men to themselves.

Ed went to the forge and heated it up, found a link to match the chain, and went to work. Jory stood by and smiled every time Ed looked his way. When Ed was finished with the little job, he held the pair of hobbles apart at chest height and said, "That's hotter'n hell. I don't know if you want to soak it in water."

"Should I?"

"Don't know about the leather."

"Won't hurt it." Jory took the hobbles.

At that moment, Ed's gaze was pulled to an image beyond the open doorway, a slender dark shape of a man crossing the street at a three-quarters profile. Ed felt the old, prickly sensation run through his upper body.

"What's the matter?" Jory's voice seemed distant.

Ed came back to himself and was surprised to see Jory standing so near. "I just saw something."

"What'd you see? You look like you saw a ghost. All the color drained out of your face."

Ed took a deep breath. "It was like a ghost, but it wasn't. It was a man walking across the street." He craned his neck to the right. "I need to see if I can get another look at him."

He went to the open doorway, with Jory half a step behind. The man was nowhere in sight.

Jory's hat appeared at the corner of Ed's vision. "See him?"

"No, he's gone for right now."

"Someone you know?"

"Someone I saw once before. A long time ago." Ed searched up and down the street, taking in men and horses and wagons, but he did not see the man he was looking for.

A few seconds later, the man appeared on the sidewalk across the street and down a ways on the left. He did not look around, nor did he seem in a hurry. He stepped down into the street, untied a sorrel horse from the hitchrack, mounted up, and rode away.

Ed's heart was beating fast. He expelled a long breath as he watched the horse and rider recede. In spite of the sounds from the rock crusher, the world seemed silent.

"Is that him?" came Jory's voice at his side.

"That's the man." Ed gave a slow shake of the head, as if to clear away any uncertainties. He turned to Jory. "Do you know who he is?"

"Two bits." Emerson's voice came out loud from behind them.

The two young men turned. Jory smiled, showing a full set of good teeth. With the hobbles dangling in his left hand, he dug into his trousers pocket and brought out a coin. As he handed it to Emerson, he said, "Much obliged."

"Not at all." Emerson lingered.

"I'll be right there," Ed told him. "Just one little thing."

Emerson turned and walked away.

Ed raised his eyebrows. "Sorry," he said. "Wasn't worth more'n a dime."

"Aw, that's all right. They didn't cost me anything."

Ed cast his glance down the street again. The stranger was nowhere in sight. Half-turning to Jory, Ed asked, "Did you say you know him?"

"Didn't say, yet. But I think I know who he is. One of Mort Ramsey's men."

"Who's that?"

"Mort Ramsey? Aw, he's got a big place out in Thunder Basin. Calls it the King Diamond Ranch."

"Thunder Basin. Where exactly is that? I've heard of it, but I've never been there."

"It's north and west of here. You go to Litch, then north from there. You get out into some pretty big country."

"Huh. I just met a girl who said she was on her way to stay in Litch. I should go there some time. How far is it?"

Jory smiled. "Oh, I don't know. Maybe a day's ride, but quite a bit less if you know a girl there."

"I don't ride like you do. I just ride gentle horses." Ed looked down the street and saw nothing in particular.

Jory's voice came in a lilt. "Someone's got to gentle 'em."

Ed turned and nodded. "Good thing." Then he saw the tripod where he had left it. "Well, I'd better get back to work."

"Good enough. I need to shove along anyway. But if you ever get out that way, don't be a stranger. Like Homer says, we'll water down the soup and put another plate on the table."

"Tompkins Ranch."

"You bet. About halfway to Litch, there's a road turns off by an old mound of dirt. They call it the Barrow. Go north twelve miles, and you're in the yard."

"I might do that."

* * * * *

Ed saw the Barrow and the road that turned there, but he kept on the trail to Litch. Maybe on the way back he would ride the twelve miles, but for the time being he wanted to see if he could make the ride to Litch in one day.

It was a good time of year to travel—not hot and not cold. The grass had greened up, and the call of meadowlarks carried on the clear air. Here and there an antelope showed, white and tan against the rolling grassland. More than once a prairie dog sat upright on the mound of its burrow and watched him from twenty feet away. In mid-afternoon he jumped a jackrabbit, lanky and long-eared. The animal bolted to the left, cut right and crossed the trail, then kept on its zig-zag way to the northwest until it disappeared behind a rise. Dawes had said that if you let out a long whistle, a jackrabbit would stop and perk up his ears to listen. Ed never tried it.

He made it to Litch when the sun was slipping in the west and he had to pull his hatbrim down, but as he rode into the main street, he put the hat in its regular position. He wanted to be noticed as little as possible, while at the same time he wanted to see as much as he could without staring.

The town had a rougher look to it than Glenrose did. Most of the buildings were weathered and unpainted, and what trees there were had not grown to eye level of a man on horseback. Most of them were elms, thin branches just leafing out.

He imagined that for Mrs. Porter to say, as she had, that her boarding house was the best by far in this town, there must be more an element of pride than a basis of comparison. He did not find the place on his first pass through, but on his way back, he found it on a cross street in the middle of the next block to the north. The sign, which hung out perpendicular from the building, had seen some weather. The white background paint was flaking, and the lower part of the "r" on "Iris" had disappeared, so that it looked like a cattle brand or a letter from a foreign language.

He tied his horse at the hitching rail and walked up the wooden steps, feeling nervous. At the desk inside, Mrs. Porter in her spectacles gave him a close look as she answered his question about staying just one night. She kept her eye on him as he signed his name in the register.

Looking straight at him, she said, "Aren't you the boy who was asking all the questions in Glenrose?"

He drew back. "Yes, I am, but I didn't know I was asking all of them."

Mrs. Porter folded her hands together on the counter. "Well, if you came here just to see her, don't get your hopes up. She's got work to do, and one rule of the house is that everyone minds his own business."

"Oh, to be sure. And as far as that goes, I didn't come this way just to see her. I'm going farther on, north of here, to see some of the country. I thought I would stay at this place, since you said it was the best in town."

"I've got no quarrel with that." She gave him another close look. "I thought you worked."

"I do. I'm taking a little time off."

"You mean you quit."

"Not exactly. Working in the shop was fine all winter, but I want to get out and see some things. I've got enough to pay my way, and if he hires someone else by the time I get back, I can find another job. I've always worked, and I'm not afraid of it."

She pushed a key toward him. "Room sixteen. You'll share it with another working man. Supper's at seven."

During the meal he caught every glimpse he could of Ravenna, her dark hair and shapely figure, but she did not linger. As she was clearing away the last of the dishes, she spoke.

"Mrs. Porter says you're passing through. I hope you have a safe journey."

"Thank you."

She did not reappear, so he left the table and went out to take the night air. He walked up and down the main street, steering wide of the saloons but catching a glimpse inside each of them. Seeing nothing to attract his interest, he went back to the boarding house.

That night he slept in a narrow room, not six feet from a man with a large belly who groaned and snored. In the morning he saw Ravenna but did not speak to her, and not long after breakfast he rode north out of Litch.

* * * * *

For the first three or four hours he did not see a tree, only plain landscape with grass, cactus, and low sagebrush. Then he came to broken country, with bulges and gashes so rough he wondered how a cowpuncher could get cattle out of them. Yet the grass sprouted green in the bottoms, and cedar trees showed up here and there.

By late afternoon, the trail rose and wound through low hills with sparse vegetation. Off to the west and north, the breaks drained toward a valley that rose on the far side to a row of bluffs. Ed followed the trail down into the valley on the right.

The hills on his left, to the northeast, had an orange hue and were dotted with dark clumps of brush, but for the most part, they were bare and set apart from one another. Then came a line of hills running south by southeast, also orange and with a liberal spacing of pine trees.

On the valley floor, out on a flat of grass and stirrup-high sagebrush, he found a waterhole. After letting his horse drink, he moved about a quarter of a mile west, where he found a low bluff and a six-foot cedar. He picketed his horse a ways off, rolled out his camp, and appreciated the silence as the shadows lengthened.

* * * * *

The sun came up early over the hills in the east, and Ed was surprised to see that the hills were now green instead of orange. He figured it must be the light.

He took the horse to water, set it out again, and boiled a cup of coffee in a can. Meadowlarks were singing, as were some small blackish birds with white shoulders, and the morning was still fresh when he saddled the horse and tied on his gear. He decided this valley was worth a look, so he marked in his mind where the main trail lay, and he set out across the landscape.

The first thing he noticed was the great number of prairie dog holes, every one of them abandoned. Most of them had drifted or washed in, and in the mouths of many of the holes, small dead tumbleweeds had settled.

Crossing the flat, he rode down into a creek bottom, where he saw the hide remnants and the scattered bones of an antelope that must have died in the winter. Past the remains, he crossed a muddy trickle and climbed out the other side. Along the flank of the hills, he saw the source of yesterday's orange. Underfoot, there lay millions of small, shaly, orange bits of flat rock that he imagined must shine brighter when the sun crossed over and hit them at a direct angle. Also on the hillside he saw chunks of sandstone, many of them that looked suitable for building banks, hotels, or ranch houses.

He rode to the top of a smooth hill, threading through pines, and there he saw the clear silhouette of a dead pine tree against the blue sky. All the needles and twigs were long gone, and the outstretched limbs were smooth and dark.

Farther along, he came to a vantage point where he could see the valley below. From camp he had seen the leafless tops of several trees, and now he saw the larger picture. A long watercourse, with a great many draws draining into it, threaded through this valley. Ed observed where the water had cut against one bank and another as the course had changed over the years. For about a mile, the banks were fifty to a hundred yards apart, and in the wide, grassy bottom, huge cottonwoods had grown. Most of them grew in clumps while a few stood alone, and almost every one was dead. Some had fallen over, showing large, uprooted trunks, and from the debris that had caught between the branches and the ground, Ed could imagine the powerful flash floods that might come through here. In spite of the wreckage, at least a hundred trees stood upright along the course, their grey and broken branches giving the place the character of an old cemetery.

On his way out of the valley, Ed stopped at the waterhole again. Then he found the trail and followed it as it wound to the north. It took him through more broken country, into a land of vast reaches where, more than a day's ride in all directions, bluffs and buttes rose in the hazy distance. He felt as if he had entered an interior country, a broad, uncharted land that lay between the old road to the east, which ran from Cheyenne to the Black Hills, and the Bozeman Trail on the west, that went to Douglas and Casper and then north from there.

From time to time the broken country would smooth out a little into a wide, grassy bowl a few miles across. In one of these, off to his left, he saw the headquarters of a ranch. It lay downslope and sheltered from north and westerly winds but uphill from the creek that ran through the drainage. A mile farther, he came to a road that led into the ranch area he had just seen. A massive gateway, made of upright logs and a crossbeam that must have been hauled a long way, marked the entrance. Hanging from the cross-member by two short chains was a plank two feet wide and about nine feet long, with the words "King Diamond Ranch" burned into the lumber.

Ed rode back along the trail until he could see the headquarters again. Here in the middle of this far-flung country called Thunder Basin, he had found the place he was looking for. He would know it when he came this way again.

* * * * *

He camped in the valley of the dead cottonwoods on his way back to Litch. The hills showed orange again, and the only difference from the evening before was the appearance of a big, feathery-legged owl that came flapping out of the bare branches of a cottonwood as he rode past.

* * * * *

He returned to Litch without having seen or talked to another human being since he left. In town once again, he checked into the Iris, where Mrs. Porter had minimal conversation and where he exchanged about as many words with Ravenna as on his previous visit. After supper he had a bath, then ended up in the room with the same man as before.

The man, who seemed inclined to talk, asked Ed if he was looking for work.

"Not quite. I did see some ranches, though. One in particular caught my eye. The King Diamond."

"Oh, yeah." The man wrinkled his nose. "I used to work there." He was sitting on the edge of his bed, and at this point he braced himself with his hands on his knees and started coughing. He hawked up a gob and spit it into a can by his foot.

"Really? How long ago was that?"

"Left about ten years ago. Worked there five years. Hasn't changed much since then, from what I've heard." The man did not seem to harbor any fond memories.

"Hmm. I was wonderin' about a fella who works there."

"Which one?"

"Thin sort of fella. Dark features, dark hat."

"Snake Eyes."

"Is that what they call him?"

"No, that's what I call him. His name is Bridge."

"Bridge, huh? Did he work there when you did?"

"Oh, yeah. Him and Ramsey go 'way back." The man coughed again. "What's your interest in him?"

"Not much. I just saw him and wondered who he was."

"Lots of things to wonder about in this life. When I was your age, I wondered about the girls and what I might get to do with them."

"Oh, I wonder about that, too."

The man held his hand on the bottom of his belly. "Well, don't worry about any of the rest of it until you have to."

"I'll try to remember that."

Ed went to sleep as soon as the man turned down the lamp. He slept straight through, and in the morning he realized the older man's snoring hadn't bothered him at all.

Chapter Three

When Ed came to the Barrow, he turned north. Twelve miles into the yard, Jory had said. It seemed like a lot of extra travel to have ridden south to Litch, east to the Barrow, and now north to the ranch. There had to be more than one way to cut across country southeast from where he had left the Thunder Basin area the day before, but until he knew the country better, he had to stick to the main roads.

As he traveled north, he thought of what kind of an impression he would make. He was riding a rented horse and saddle, and he didn't have a rifle, pistol, or rope. He wasn't a greenhorn in a derby hat and city suit, but he didn't look like a range rider, either, and that was what he decided he wanted to be. In his way of thinking, it would be the best way to get him onto the King Diamond Ranch.

He turned his gaze outward, observing the landscape he rode through. It was like much of what he had seen in the last few days—hilly grassland with low sagebrush and prickly pear cactus, open range with cattle in small bunches.

The land seemed to make a gradual rise, though it was hard to tell when he went up one hillside and down the other. When he came to a rise and looked around, however, he could see farther to the south than to the north. It was a peaceful country, with the song of the meadowlarks tinkling, the touch of a breeze on his face, and the smell of sage.

Onward he rode. The sun warmed his back and made the neck of the sorrel horse shine. Little heat waves danced in the distance. He came to a low ridge that ran east and west and had pine trees growing along the flank. There he rested in the shade of one of the larger pines, sitting on a rock with his hat in one hand and the reins in the other.

After a long moment, he realized he was staring at an anthill, a domed structure about four feet across and a foot and a half high, a patchwork of twigs and grass and pine needle fragments. About two hundred yards away, he saw another, and off in the opposite direction, he saw another. These were different from the ones he had seen in Thunder Basin, which were lower and straight-sloped, like a broad cone or the thin breast of a young girl. They had consisted of rock granules, mostly dark but other shades as well and had four feet of bare earth all the way around. Here, the shaggy domes rose out of the grass and sagebrush.

Past the pine ridge, the country rolled away a little flatter than before. The sorrel horse kept picking up his feet and moving along at a fast walk, tossing his head once in a while but giving no trouble. The land seemed to rise again, and when the sun was a couple of hours past the meridian, Ed came to a rise and stopped. The horse could use a breather, and Ed wanted a moment to take in the landscape.

A broad, rich-looking grassland stretched away and leveled out for a couple of miles all the way around. The grass seemed a deeper green, and it rippled in the slight breeze. Off to the left, a ridge of low buttes formed a natural boundary, as did a chalky-looking row of bluffs to the right. Straight ahead, a massive butte rose as the backdrop for a set of ranch buildings. Ed had come to know that a large landmark such as this one was often much farther away than it looked, and from the size of the buildings, he guessed he was between two and three miles from the ranch.

His eyes returned to the butte. The dark trees that terraced the upper half of it were small as well. The very top of the formation, which slanted downward from left to right, was bare and jagged. Then came the trees, tesselated, and in the lower half as the base sloped out, the grass grew as dark as on the surrounding plain.

The sorrel horse must have had a good idea that the day's travel was coming to an end, for he made short work of the last stretch of trail. As Ed approached the ranch headquarters, on the right sat a two-story house, all of lumber and painted white. Across the hard-packed yard from it squatted a long, low, weathered structure that he imagined had been built in two sections. As each half had a stovepipe sticking out of the roof, Ed took this building to be the bunkhouse and kitchen. Straight ahead, with the butte still a half-mile in the background, rose a barn with a gambrel roof and hayloft. A set of corrals reached out on either side of the barn, while farther back on the left, a grove of cottonwoods showed their bright, rustling leaves. A barking dog appeared at the doorway of the barn, followed by a man in the hat and clothes of a ranch hand.

The man stepped out into the light and waited as Ed rode past the ranch house and dismounted. Leading the horse, he went forward, glad to be getting his feet back on the ground after the last couple of hours in the saddle.

"How-do," called out the cowpuncher, in a voice that was not young.

"Afternoon. Is this the Tompkins Ranch?"

"Sure is." The man set his hat back above his forehead, showing a ridge of dark hair that lightened to grey as it faded at his temples.

"Jory told me that if I was ever out this way I should drop in, so I did."

"That's fine," said the older man. "He's out tryin' to break his neck, but he should be back pretty soon." He looked at the sorrel, then at Ed, with pale blue eyes that looked as if they had been washed out by years of sunlight. "I'd guess you'll stay over."

"If it's all right."

"Of course." The man glanced again at the horse. "Let's put him away." He went to turn, then stopped, pivoted, and put out his hand. "By the way, I'm Homer. No sense bein' a stranger." Friendly creases came to his face as he smiled.

As they shook, Ed smiled and nodded. "I'm Edward Dawes. Just call me Ed."

"Good enough." Homer led the way into the barn, where he gave the horse a scoop of oats as Ed went about unsaddling. When he lifted the saddle and blankets clear, Homer showed him a rack where he could put the gear.

Hoofbeats sounded as a horse came into the yard at a trot. The dog pushed up from the floor where it had been watching Ed. It padded to the doorway but did not bark. Ed followed.

He watched as Jory Stoner swung down from a tall roan and, reins in hand, loosened the rear and then the front cinch. Jory was all cowboy, from his spurs to his broad-brimmed hat.

"That's a big horse," Ed called out.

Jory looked around, and his face broke into a smile. "What do you know? I didn't expect to see you this soon."

"Oh, I took some time off."

"Go to see the girl in Litch?"

"Just barely."

"Did you meet Homer?"

"He helped me put my horse away."

"That's good." Jory led the big roan forward, stopped at the hitching rail, and held out the reins. "Here," he said. "I'll unsaddle him out here. He's still a little green." He turned to the horse and patted the dappled neck, then unbuckled the cinches in the same order as he had loosened them before. Patting the horse on the rump, he walked around to the other side, where he lifted the leather rear cinch and the woven front cinch and draped them across the saddle. Then he came back to the left side, and as the tall horse stood trembling, he slid the saddle, pad, and blanket from the animal's back. He let out a sigh of relief, and still leaning backward, he carried the gear into the barn. He came back with a brush, and with one hand on the horse, he gave it a brushing. By the time he was done, the animal had relaxed. Jory handed the brush to Ed and took the reins. "I'll put him away, and then we'll see if Homer needs anything."

After the boys had pitched hay and washed up at the pump, they went to the bunkhouse. Homer, who had gone ahead, had a fire going in the cookstove. His hat hung on the wall, and his hair was combed.

"When it's just me and Jory," he said, "I wrangle the spuds and biscuits. When the boss puts on a few more hands, he gets a cook."

"Does the boss live in the other house?"

"That's right. Him and his wife and his kids." Homer rapped the poker on one of the removable plates of the stovetop, and it settled into place. "He's all right. This is a good outfit. Say, you'd best bring in your gear if you're goin' to spend the night."

After a supper of fried bacon and potatoes, Jory washed the dishes while Homer rolled a cigarette and smoked it. Ed noticed that whatever the older man did, he did not move fast but his hands were sure.

Tipping his ash in a sardine can, Homer raised his eyebrows. "So, have you been out to see the country?"

"A little bit of it."

"He's from Glenrose," Jory said over his shoulder. "Knows a girl in Litch."

Homer gave a wry smile. "That must be a better place than here, then."

"In some ways, maybe."

Jory spoke again. "This is the boy who fixed the hobbles for me."

"Oh, then you work in the blacksmith shop."

"Not right now. Well, I could go back, I guess, but I'm thinkin' of tryin' something else."

Jory flashed his smile. "In Litch?"

"That's not my idea." Ed hesitated, then went ahead. "What I'd like to do is learn how to do this kind of work."

"Punchin' cows?" Homer stopped with the cigarette halfway to his lips.

"That's right. The kind of work you fellas do."

Homer took a drag and blew out the smoke. "What the hell you want to do somethin' like that for?"

"So I can get a job wherever I go."

"Blacksmithin's a better trade, really, and it pays through the winter. But I 'magine you want to ride fast horses and not be tied down all the time. Drift when you want."

Jory spoke up again. "Maybe he wants to be closer to Litch."

"That might be part of it."

Homer raised his eyebrows again. "Do you have an outfit in mind to go to work for, over that way?"

"Not yet." Ed shifted in his seat. "I was wonderin' if there was any possibility of my gettin' on here."

"Here?" said Jory.

"Well, if it's not too far out of the question. I might be new to cow-punchin', but I've been around horses, especially at the blacksmith shop, and whatever else I know about iron work can't hurt."

Jory laughed. " 'Less you get caught with a runnin' iron."

"No," said Homer, "you don't want to be carryin' one of them under your saddle skirts."

"Be sure I won't. Besides, I grew up doin' all kinds of farm work as well. I'm no stranger to an axe or a shovel. 'Course, it's this other stuff I want to get handy at."

"Well, if you wanta be a cah-boy," said Homer, with a bit of a drawl, "there's worse places to learn. I can teach you to keep from trippin' over your spurs, and Jory can teach you to git back up when you fall off a horse. But you'll have to ask the boss."

* * * * *

In the morning, Ed saddled up and went out with Jory to bring in a string of horses. They rode toward the east end of the high butte, where the horses grazed in a fenced-in pasture. In the middle of the pasture, with nothing but grassland all around, two cottonwood trees about twelve feet high grew out of the bermed side of a man-made pond. Light from the rising sun tinged the green leaves with gold, and the refracted light sparkled on the surface of the pond. Beyond the trees, the bell on the lead horse tinkled. For a moment the world seemed like a peaceful, benevolent place until the shapes of two dark horses, one standing beyond and at a right angle to the other, look like a horse and rider. The illusion lasted but a second, but it brought to mind a word that Ed had already run through his head a hundred times. *Bridge*.

"Hep, hep," said Jory, putting his horse into a trot. "Let's get 'em goin'."

Ed gave his horse a nudge as well, and within a couple of seconds, the other eight horses all had their heads raised and turned like a herd of deer.

"Just follow us," Jory called out as his horse moved into a lope. He rode toward the loose horses, veered around to his left, made a half-circle, and headed back to the ranch. He had picked up the lead horse, a big-chested bay, along with a short-eared sorrel that stayed close, and the rest of the string fell in. Jory rode ahead at a gallop, and the drumming of horse hooves sounded like soft thunder as the eight horses floated behind and raised a low cloud of dust. The magic of the morning had returned, and Ed's heart was light as he loped his horse behind the others.

The boss was sitting at the table when the boys returned to the bunkhouse for breakfast. He stood up and gave Ed a quick looking-over as he held out his hand and introduced himself.

"Cal Tompkins."

"Edward Dawes."

"Sit down and have your breakfast. Homer was just telling me about his life among the sheepherders."

"Damn short story," said Homer.

The boss sat down at his side of the table, and the two boys sat opposite him. From the first moment, Ed formed a favorable impression of Cal Tompkins. The man was clean-shaven and clear-eyed, with a healthy complexion. He wore a brown leather vest over a clean grey work shirt; his worn leather gloves lay on the crown of a dove-colored hat, which sat on the table next to him. A canvas jacket hung on the back of a chair, also to the man's left.

Homer set a plate of flapjacks on the table. "Hope these aren't too cold."

"Couldn't be," said Jory, smiling. "Not if you made 'em today." He reached his plate near and flipped three of the six onto it.

"Dig in," said Homer. "I've got enough batter for a couple more. There's molasses."

Ed served himself and waited for the jar of dark stuff.

Cal Tompkins spoke up. "Homer says you want to see if you can make a hand."

Ed met the man's steady eye. "That's right."

"Says you know a little bit."

"I grew up doin' farm work, so I've been around animals. And I've worked in a blacksmith shop."

"Do you know how to shoe horses?"

"A little bit, but I'm not an expert."

Tompkins laughed. "That's pretty good. Some fellas, when they want a job, will say, 'Oh, sure,' and then leave you with a lame horse. What else?"

"Like I told Homer, I'm not afraid to work with an ax or a shovel or a pitchfork."

"That's all right, too. Do you have a saddle?"

"Not yet."

"You can use one of these. There's plenty."

Ed's pulse was picking up. "That would be swell."

Tompkins nodded. "We can give it a try, then. Can you start in a week?"

"I can start sooner. Just as soon as I can get to town and back."

"Well, the season—that is, the pay period—starts on the twenty-fifth. If you want to come sooner to get your feet wet, that would be all right. By the way, how do you think you'll get here?"

"I haven't thought about that yet, but I'll get here. I'll walk if I have to."

Tompkins laughed again. "You don't have to do that. Jory can go in with you, take an extra horse. There's a couple things he can pick up for me while he's at it. By the way, have you ever been in jail?"

Ed frowned. "No, why?"

"I need someone to tell Jory what it's like."

Jory handed Ed the molasses. "You'll learn to know when he's kiddin'. Every time I go to town, he warns me about gettin' thrown in jail."

The boss smiled. "You boys have a good time, but don't stay more than one night. You know how Homer worries."

Homer set two coffee cups on the table. "Ever since my life among the missionaries."

* * * * *

With the coils in his left hand and the loop in his right, Ed swung his rope three times and made his toss. With his feet on the ground and the stump only ten feet away, he thought it should be easier, but the hondo, or eye of the loop, slapped against the edge of the stump and bounced aside. Ed pulled in the rope and shook out another loop. With his hands lowered, he took a deliberate breath and exhaled. In a few days he was going to be on a moving horse, throwing at moving cattle, so he had better learn to throw the loop while it was still easy.

Later that day, he saddled the horse he had ridden from town. With the rope tied onto the right side, he headed out to the pasture northwest of the corrals. The horse kept at a steady walk and did not flinch when Ed took down the rope and started swinging a loop. Here came a little sagebrush, about the size of a calf's head. Not this one. Too close in. Ed looked down at it as he rode by. When the next one came up, he threw his loop and missed. The horse kept walking and was well past the bush when Ed pulled up the curled end of his rope.

He built another loop, and then another, and a half-dozen more until he settled one around a bush that looked like all the others. Satisfied, he gave a pull to his slack, then tried to shake it out again. The loop stayed the same, snug around the bush. He shook again, and the horse kept walking. He could think of only one thing—trying to get the rope loose—but it wasn't getting any better, and the rope was warming his hands as it slid through. When it paid out all the way, it fell to the ground, and he realized he could have stopped the horse at any point and dismounted, which was what he was going to have to do anyway. He huffed a short breath and reined the horse around. No one had seen him drop the rope, so that was good, and at least he had made a catch.

* * * * *

More than fifty horses milled in the big corral, kicking up dust. Jory and Homer had brought in the horse herd, and as Jory explained, each man was in charge of his own string. He would begin by getting to know them, combing out each one and getting him used to the halter again. Then came the bridle and saddle.

"Some'll eat pie out of your hand," Jory said, "and some'll toss you in the rocks and cactus just for the pure fun of it."

After a few tries, Ed began to get the hang of roping out horses. It wasn't like tossing down at a stump or sagebrush. He had to throw high and try to guess where the horse was going to turn its head. Some, of course, he could walk up to, but others liked to play the game every time.

His favorite was a little bay, reddish-brown with a coarse black mane and tail. Jory said the horse had been called Punkin before, but Ed could name him whatever he wanted. Punkin was good enough.

Ed knew he couldn't get too sweet on this one, though, because he was going to have to ride each one when its turn came. He didn't trust the white one with black flecks. It tried to reach around to bite him when he tightened the cinch, which wasn't much trouble when he had the horse snubbed close, but when he led him out and went to give it another pull, he had to keep a lookout.

"Don't let him do that," said Jory.

"How do I keep him from it?"

"Punch him."

Another horse that Ed had his doubts about was a husky dark horse. Its coat varied from dull black to dark brown, and it had a thick black mane and tail. When Ed took him out for a ride, the horse would break into a run for no apparent reason. Then he took to bolting when Ed threw his leg over the saddle and hadn't caught the right stirrup yet. It was all Ed could do to hang on until he reined the horse in.

"He's got a lot of fresh on him," said Jory. "He'll come around."

* * * * *

On the twenty-fourth, the day before the work season began, Cal Tompkins brought in four more men. Two were brothers named McLaughlin, who kept to themselves. One was a man a few years older than Ed or Jory; his name was Jeff, and he said he was from Arkansas. The fourth was a short, bald, pot-bellied man named Reuben, who came to cook. He had been coming to the ranch for a few years, so he took over with full authority. He put Ed to peeling spuds and the McLaughlin brothers to rustling firewood. That night he served fried beefsteak, and when Jeff pushed back his plate at the end of the meal and said it was pretty damn good, Reuben's face stiffened.

"It better be. And put your plate in the wreck pan before you sit back on your ass and smoke a cigarette."

Jeff paused as he was drawing out a bag of Bull Durham. The features in his face seemed to lower about an inch, but he did as he was told. Then he rolled his smoke, lit it, and started talking about hunting wild turkey.

Homer said he favored roasted duck.

Jeff tipped his head up. "Duck or goose, especially your barnyard types, are a little too greezy for me. 'Sides, I like to go out and hunt my own."

"They do that here," said Homer.

"Wild turkey?"

"Not so much. Mostly other men's beef."

Jory and Ed laughed, but the McLaughlin brothers kept quiet and didn't look up from rolling their cigarettes.

Jeff said, "I've heard of that," and he seemed to Ed like the type who liked to get in the last word.

* * * * *

All six of the ranch hands went to working with their horses the next morning. Ed was glad he had a few days' start when he saw how handy the three new fellows were. The McLaughlin brothers, bird-faced and quiet, roped out their horses with a keen eye and a deft hand. Jeff had a looser style, but when he slapped on a saddle and pulled the cinches, Ed could see he was showing the horse who was boss.

By the second day, each man was to have ridden all the horses in his string. Only one man at a time could take a horse into the round pen, and the others were spread out so as not to get in one another's way. As the day was warming up after noon dinner, Ed roped the dark horse and led him out of the corral. He got the saddle and bridle on all right, then walked the horse out so he could tighten the cinch another notch or two. He also wanted to stay out of the way in case the animal bolted when he swung aboard.

That was exactly what the horse did. It broke into a dead run before Ed could get his right foot into the stirrup, and he had to hang onto the saddle horn and clamp with his leg to keep from being jolted off. The horse was heading for open country, while Ed was getting banged up and still couldn't catch his stirrup. With his right hand he pulled the slack in his reins, and with his left he tried to rein the animal in. When the horse didn't slow, Ed pulled harder. Then the animal bunched up, and the real trouble began.

When the horse had been running, Ed had been looking out over his low head, but now he was looking down into the dark swirls of mane. He tried to grab the saddle horn with his right hand, but the bucking fit continued. The fury and the force were tremendous. Still pulling on the reins with his left hand, Ed found the saddle horn with his right, then lost it, got knocked against the swells like before, smashed his left hand on something hard, and went flying off to the right. The ground came up to meet him, hard, as he landed on his hip and right arm. He felt the horse step on his legs, and then he was alone, lying in the dirt by a clump of sagebrush, still wearing his hat.

He pushed himself up onto his hands and knees and saw the horse about seventy yards away, reins on the ground as he stood in profile watching the man rise from the dirt. Wavering, Ed stood up and tested his legs. His right knee hurt like hell, but he could walk. The last two knuckles on his left hand had swollen up, and the fingers didn't move very well.

He knew he was supposed to get back on the horse. First he had to catch him. With slow steps he moved toward the animal, keeping his eye on the front quarter. The horse moved, stepped on a rein, and stopped. Ed walked up to it and took the reins.

The horse would not let him on. Each time Ed raised his boot to the stirrup, the horse moved away sideways. After a few attempts, Ed walked the horse in a circle and tried again. The horse still moved aside. Ed tried the routine a few more times, but he felt so beaten up that he had to lead the horse back to the yard.

Jory stood with his thumbs in his belt as Ed came limping in. "Pitched a fit, did he?"

Ed held up his left hand, which had a big round swelling by now. "Banged me up pretty good. Stepped on my leg, too. At least the right one. I tried to get back on, but he wouldn't let me, and I was beat to hell."

"Sometimes you just can't. At least you're walkin'."

* * * * *

Ed lay on his bunk the rest of that day and through the next. He had purple-and-blue bruises on his inner thighs, a bruise like a purple-and-red plum on his right knee, a scrape on his left shin, an aching big toe, and smaller sores and bruises along his arms. The swelling on his left hand had gone down a little, but he still couldn't find the last knuckle.

"You'll be fine," said Homer. "You're young, and nothing's broke. It could have been a lot worse."

On the second day after his wreck, he was able to hobble up and down the length of the bunkhouse, though the step down to go out back caused him a shooting pain in his right leg.

The bruises on his knee and thighs spread and met in a blotchy mass. He was worried at the bruises getting larger instead of smaller, and then they started to dull in color. He figured the best thing he could do was move around, so he hobbled from his bunk to the kitchen and back every hour or so.

Reuben, the cook, sat and smoked a cigarette. "That's what old age is going to be like," he said.

"I don't want to think about old age."

"Maybe you won't have to."

The next day, the bruises were starting to turn yellow on the edges and in the thin spots. On the day after that, some of the splotches were becoming speckles. When Homer asked him how he was doing, he said it was starting to itch.

"That's good. When it starts to itch, that means it's startin' to get better."

Ed opened and closed his left hand. It was all vivid to him—the desire to stay on a threshing animal, the need to ride it out, and the knowledge that he had to get back on when he could. "This thing still hurts," he said, "and so does my knee, but I'm goin' to get back on that horse, even if someone has to hold him for me."

Homer smiled. "That's the way to make a hand."

Chapter Four

With four coils in his left hand and the tail of the rope dangling toward his boot, Ed leaned into the wind and swung his loop. Punkin the bay horse was on his smooth, dead run, eating up the ground between him and the steer. Ed felt at one with the horse, his balance perfect and the purpose clear. As the horse's right shoulder came even with the steer's left hip, Ed threw his loop, aiming at the tip of the steer's right horn. The loop settled over the horns and hung on the tip of the steer's nose, then moved an inch back. Ed jerked his slack, slowed the horse, took his dallies, and turned the steer.

The animal fought, shaking its head and planting its feet, but the little bay horse leaned into the job and pulled the steer skipping back to the herd. Once there, Ed tried to shake the loop off the horns, but it stayed put. Bill McLaughlin rode close, leaned down, and pulled it off.

"Little sumbitch doesn't want to stay with us," he said. "Who knows but he'll try to leave in the night."

Ed nodded thanks and turned away, hauling in his rope as he went back to his place. With twenty-seven head and five riders, a fellow would think they had things sewn up pretty well, but this was the fourth or fifth time the steer had tried to break away.

Tompkins had sent everyone but Jory to pick up these cattle that were held over from a roundup farther south, and it was a two-day job to trail them back to the ranch. Homer said he had a good place picked out to camp overnight, but Ed didn't look forward to trying to keep the little herd together during the night.

On through the hot afternoon they rode, with the herd strung out nearly a hundred yards. Bill McLaughlin took it upon himself to ride herd on the unruly steer, and every time it tried to cut loose, he was right on it, slapping it in the face with his rope and hazing it back to the herd.

In the late afternoon, Homer led them half a mile west to a muddy little waterhole. Not far away was an outcropping of ancient mud that would give shelter against anything that came out of the west. The McLaughlin brothers held back and watched the cattle crowd around the water while the other three riders went to the camp site.

"Look out for snakes," said Homer. "This is always a good place for 'em."

Jeff dismounted with his lariat in hand and began stalking the area. He had a distinctive way of walking, with the tips of his boots pointed outward, and he was a little heavy around the middle, so it looked as if his weight shifted back and forth from one foot to another. At the edge of the bare spot, close to the base of the little bluff, he stopped and squared off. Holding a big loop as if he were about to rope heels, he brought the lariat up and around and swatted at the ground. He slapped another half-dozen times with the braided rawhide whistling and thudding. With the toe of his boot, he lifted a medium-sized snake and sent it on a low trajectory into the sagebrush.

Homer, resting his rein hand on the saddle horn, turned to Ed. "If you don't have that habit, you'd just as well not pick it up."

"Killin' snakes?"

"With a rope."

Jeff went after his horse, which he had left ground-hitched. The animal had flinched at the first sounds of the lariat but had stayed put.

A little later on, as Ed was coaxing a fire out of a small heap of sagebrush, Jeff spoke up.

"What's wrong with killin' snakes?"

"Nothin'," said Homer. "I just wouldn't do it with a rope."

"Rawhide's pretty hard. Works good."

"I wouldn't want the chance of pickin' up a fang when I was pullin' the rope back in."

"I had leather gloves on."

"That's fine," said Homer. "You do what you want. I don't know if it's true, but I've heard of a fang goin' through thicker leather than that."

Ed looked up and raised his eyebrows, as a way of saying he was interested in the story.

Homer went on. "Like a lot of tales, this one came out of Texas. The way it goes, a young fella died after killin' a snake, but they couldn't find any bites on him, and they didn't know what killed him. His brother inherited his boots, which were in a lot better shape than his own, and not long after he took to wearin' 'em, damn if he didn't die, too. Well, what with the boots bein' the one thing in common, the other fellas looked 'em over, and they found a rattlesnake fang right here in the crease." Homer pointed at his own boot.

"Sounds to me like a tall tale from Texas." Jeff pulled out his tobacco sack and crinkled his nose.

"Might be," said Homer, "but I wouldn't want to push my luck around rattlers."

Thick smoke was coming out of the nest of dry sagebrush, so Ed took off his hat and fanned air into the base. A small blaze leapt up, and the smoke cleared. Ed pushed himself back onto his heels and stood up, then looked around at the McLaughlin brothers.

"Are they gonna stay on shift for a while?" he asked.

"Sure," said Homer. "Get yourself some rest in the meanwhile."

* * * * *

They crossed the trail from Glenrose to Litch at mid-morning the next day. Ed glanced at the Barrow, a quarter mile to his left, and remembered the first time he had seen it. He hoped that the next time he went past it to the west, he would have a better reception in Mrs. Porter's self-acclaimed boarding house.

In the afternoon, they pushed the cattle up and over the pine ridge, where Ed saw the domed anthills and thought again of his first trip this way. The weather was hotter now, the days longer. He had been through his first payday and fitted himself out with spurs and a six-gun. Jeff still treated him as if he had just been weaned, especially when they shot cans in back of the barn, but Ed knew he was making progress.

* * * * *

The men had sat down at the mess table and were waiting for Reuben to bring on the pot of beans when the storm announced itself. It began with a patter of heavy raindrops, then a strong wind and the rattle of pellets on the roof and back wall.

"Sounds like hail," said Jory. He stood up, went to the back door, and opened it. A rush of cool air came in, and water was already running off the roof in a curtain. "Sure is," he said, slamming the door.

The rattling sound became steadier and louder. Everyone got up from the table and went to stand about six feet from the back window. Marble-sized hailstones were coming in at a slant and whacking on the window, while farther out, they struck and bounced two feet up from the ground.

Jeff moved to the edge of the window and looked out to the side. "Good thing we got in," he said. "That would sting like hell."

Homer cleared his throat. "I wouldn't stand too close to the glass."

Jeff ignored him and hooked his thumbs in his belt.

The storm seemed to be picking up. The hail was falling in a thick and steady racket, but Ed could see through the window that bigger stones were coming in the midst of all the smaller ones. As big around as hen's eggs, they came at irregular intervals, thudding against the roof and wall. *Smash, smash-smash, smash-smash-smash, smash.*

Everyone had moved back from the window, and the hailstones big and little were visible as they came driven by the wind. Some of the stones hit the glass and made slush, while others bounced off.

The window crashed, and a ball of ice landed on the floor. The irregular impacts continued on the wall and roof, still with the background of the steady *rat-tat-tat* of the smaller stones. Another hailstone, round and white as a China doorknob, smashed through what was left of the window pane.

Within half an hour, the storm had passed over. The men put on their hats and went outside. The sky had cleared, and the sun had not yet touched the western rim. Sunlight poured through the calm, clean air, though a chill hung there as well. Hailstones lay in a carpet all around and in a long heap at the base of the bunkhouse. Ed picked up a larger one and looked it over. It seemed like strange fruit, a frozen white spherical berry composed of a cluster of tiny balls. He dropped it in a mound of slush.

Out front, Tompkins and his wife and two little children were standing in the yard. The little boy, who was about six years old, was holding up a hailstone that covered his palm. A black-and-white puppy was looking up at the boy's hand.

Mrs. Tompkins took the little girl inside, leaving her husband and son to the company of the men.

"If it's not too much trouble," said the boss, "you could take a look around and see if anything needs fixin' tonight."

Down by the barn and corrals, water was running toward the grove of cottonwoods. Closer to the barn, a bird nest lined with horsehair and dried grass had fallen from an elm, and the drowned little birds lay with their buggy eyes closed and their beaks opened.

"This isn't so bad," said Jeff, rocking along in his usual gait. "I've seen jackrabbits brained by hailstones as big as your fist."

Leaves and twigs lay all over the ground within forty yards of the cottonwoods, but in the wide distance beyond, the clear, blue sky seemed as innocent as ever.

* * * * *

Ed sat back on his bunk, half-watching and half-listening as Jory, Homer, and Jeff played dominoes. Before the rest of the crew arrived, Jory and Homer played cribbage of an evening, as Ed didn't care for table games. He did sit by and enjoy the talk, though. Now with Jeff in the company, it was not so pleasant, so Ed tried to keep his distance. He wasn't the only one. Just that evening, Jeff tried to get a five- or six-handed poker game going, but the McLaughlin brothers kept to themselves as always, and Reuben said he was saving up to go see the Queen of England.

"Friend of yours?" said Jeff, with his usual tinge of sarcasm.

"Not yet." Reuben widened his nostrils. "But when she gets to know me, she'll probably want me to stay."

"You'd have to learn to play whist or quadrille."

Reuben tapped his ashes. "Who says I don't know already?"

Jeff turned and said, "How about you, Ed? Play some poker?"

"Not my game."

"Well," said Jeff, "I guess we can play dominoes, then."

The game got under way as it often did, with a mixing and clattering of tiles and a running line of table talk.

"Who's got the box-car?" asked Jeff. "Whoever's got the double six, start things out." He had names for the other doubles as well—fifty-five, forty-four, thirty-three, twenty-two, snake eyes. For the tile that had two blanks, he called it "double nuts."

"No one's got it?" said Homer. "We'll start with the double five, then."

"Fifty-five. Somebody's little sister. Your turn, Jory."

When the next round began, Homer laid out the double six. "Here's the mule," he said.

"Box-car." Jeff drummed his fingers on the table.

Reuben, who was sitting at the end of the table and rolling another cigarette, looked up with his annoyed expression. "You've got to name everything, don't you?"

"What do you mean? That's its name."

"Homer says 'mule,' and you've got to cover it with 'box-car,' like one dog pissin' on top of where another did."

"Oh, let's keep it calm," said Homer. "It's just a game. Who cares what you call 'em. I called it a mule because that's what the Mexicans call it. *Mula*. They call it other things, too. The fat lady from Mahuarichi."

Jory laughed. "I never heard that one."

Jeff clacked a tile on the table. "Go ahead and play, Jory. It's your turn."

The game went on, and talk drifted from one topic to another. It came around to boxing. Jory said there had been a kid here the year before who liked to practice with the gloves.

"Oh, yeah," said Reuben. "He was good at it, too. Good to watch. Those gloves are still around, aren't they?"

"Sure." Jory looked up from the table. "How about you, Jeff? Did you ever go in for that?"

Jeff shook his head. "Not where I come from. They fight for real there."

Reuben piped up. "Arkansas, isn't it?"

"That's right."

Jory turned away from the table. "How about you, Ed? You ever practice with the gloves?"

"Nah."

"Like to try?"

"Not really."

"It's all just in fun, you know."

"Maybe it is, but I don't see any fun in it."

Jory shrugged. "That's all right."

Jeff came back into the conversation. "Ed doesn't like to have fun."

Homer frowned at his domino tiles. "Different people's got different ideas about what's fun."

Jeff had his head raised in a challenging posture. "From what I've seen, Ed doesn't like to have fun."

Ed could feel resentment welling up, but he said, "That's for me to worry about."

"Doesn't like to play cribbage, play poker, play dominoes. 'Don't see any fun in it.' That's a moper. Sit and sulk."

"Maybe I've got things to think about."

"Ed the thinker. I hadn't seen that before."

"Oh, go easy," said Homer.

"Yeah," Reuben chimed in. "Leave him alone. Maybe he's got a little girl somewhere."

"Hah. Mopers of that kind, if they think they've got a girl to moon over, it's usually some cheap little jane that spread her legs for 'em for a dollar."

Ed came off his bunk and stood in his stocking feet. He could feel his blood boiling, and he had a sense of everyone, including the McLaughlin brothers in the background, waiting to see what he was going to do.

"Jeff," he said, "you've got a big mouth."

"Aw, you rile too easy."

"You smart off too much. That's what the problem is." Ed had his fists clenched and caught himself from taking a step forward.

Jeff stood up, scraping his chair back. He had a hard, menacing look on his face. "Look here, kid. You might be as strong as the village blacksmith, but you've got a lot to learn."

"And who's gonna teach it to me?"

"Don't push too hard to find out."

Homer and Jory had stood up by now. "Now look here, both of you," said Homer. "I may not be able to whip either of you, but I'll tell you one thing. One rule on this place is there's no fightin'. The boss finds out there's been a fight, and both of you are gone, no questions asked. And it's just as well. No good comes of it."

Jeff leaned his bulk forward. "We can settle this ourselves," he said. "Without the gloves, out back."

Homer shook his head. "Make no mistake. If there's a fight, I'll tell the boss myself. I can't fire someone, but it's my job to tell the boss so he can."

Jory walked over to Ed and patted him on the shoulder. "Let it go, Ed. Don't get all worked up."

"I don't like someone talkin' that way."

"Neither do I, but I can let it pass. You, though, you're like a steam engine. You let things build up. You're natural for blow-ups."

Ed laughed. "Me? I'm the one that wants to ride tame horses."

"Oh, that's different," Jory said with a smile. "I see some fun in that."

* * * * *

Ed was walking the speckled horse past the Tompkins house when the little boy called out to him.

"Hey, puncher!"

Ed stopped and faced the kid, who for once didn't have anything in his hands. Whenever Ed had seen him before, he had been playing with the puppy, dangling a cat against his chest, or swinging a stick. Now the kid just squinted at the puncher.

"You want to see me climb this tree?" The boy pointed at a slender cottonwood about eight feet tall.

As soon as the branches forked, which was about three feet up, the tree didn't look like much for climbing, but Ed imagined it seemed huge to this little kid. "I don't know," he said.

"Watch me climb it. I'm going to go to the tippy-tippy-top."

Ed cast a dubious glance at the thin branches. "Why don't you ask your ma?"

"I'm going to climb it."

Ed didn't like the prospect, but he didn't want to put a hand on the boss's kid, so he stood there and said, "I don't know if you should."

The boy was quicker than Ed expected. He marched over to the tree, reached up to the forked branches, pulled himself up, got his feet under him, and grabbed the spindly center branch above his head. As he gave a pull, the branch bent over to his right, and he spilled nearly head first out of the tree. He hit the ground with a loud thump, and he came up right away, red-faced and screaming bloody murder.

The child's mother came running out in her apron. "Joey! Joey!" she cried. "What happened?" She knelt and took the crying boy to her chest and shoulder, where she patted his back and looked across him at the hired man. "What happened?" she asked again.

"Well, it all went so fast. I was walkin' by with this horse, and the boy said he was going to climb this tree. I told him he should ask you, but next thing I knew, he shinnied right up and fell out."

"Oh, Joey," she said, laying her cheek against the child's head. "You could hurt yourself." She raised her eyes to Ed again.

"I'm sorry," he said. "He just—"

"Don't worry. I know you didn't do anything. He was just trying to show off for you."

She took the child into the house, and Ed went on his way with the speckled horse. As he thought of the incident, two things impressed him. For one, he hadn't felt very sorry at all, and the kid's cries had been only noise to him. For another, he could not remember a woman ever holding him like that—not Mrs. Dawes, and not in the time before Pa-Pa fell in the snow that day.

* * * * *

In spite of the slow, cold rain that had been falling for two days, the bunkhouse had a cheery atmosphere. A fire blazed in the open-mouthed cast-iron stove, and a good stack of dry firewood sat in the corner. The smell of fried beefsteak hung in the room. The McLaughlin brothers had their sock feet up on empty chairs and were picking their teeth. Jory Stoner was standing near the kitchen door, where he had a ring tied to a nail on the door frame, and from the ring he worked moving backwards, braiding three long strings of leather into a cord. Homer, clean-shaven and with his hair combed, sat on the other side of the stove drinking a cup of coffee. Ed sat back a few feet so as not to point his six-gun at anyone as he oiled it.

Up and down the room, draped on empty chairs and across cots, wool and leather articles lay out to dry—gloves, chaps, holsters, scabbards. Five pairs of boots, each pair where its owner found a space, were pointed toward the stove.

Reuben came out of the kitchen with a cup of coffee and pulled up a chair for himself. "I wonder if Jeff got wet," he said.

Homer blew steam from his coffee cup. "Oh, I imagine."

Reuben made a small spitting sound, as if he were getting rid of a fleck of tobacco or a grain of coffee. "Impatient sort. Money must burn a hole in his pocket."

"Summer wages," said Homer.

"Sure, the season's over, but he could have waited out the weather like these other fellas are doin'. What's the hurry?" Reuben took up the poker and flipped a stick into the middle of the fire. "Grub's free."

Jory turned from his work and smiled. "He wants to get a bunch of cold water down the back of his neck, I say go ahead and let him do it."

"I suppose." Reuben gave a small rap with the poker on the cast-iron mouth of the stove. "What are you braidin', anyway?"

"Leather."

"I can see that, but what for?"

"Just practicin'."

Homer spoke again. "Jory's gonna find a princess whose hair reaches the back of her knees, and he's gonna spend the winter braidin' it."

Jory raised his eyebrows as he flashed his smile. "I might."

The room went quiet for a few minutes until Reuben set his coffee cup on the floor, rose from his seat, and went to the back door. He coughed and cleared his throat, then opened the door and spit outside.

The sound of soft, falling rain came in through the open door, along with a draft of cold air. Reuben closed the door. "Still comin' down," he said. "I'm glad I'm not out in it."

"Good time of year," said Homer. "Slow rain, soaks in good. Not too long after it clears out, we'll have a good frost and kill off the bugs. Horses like it."

Reuben sat down and put his hands to the fire. Looking over at the McLaughlin brothers, he said, "I bet you boys are glad you don't have to sleep out in this weather."

"We've done it," said Bill.

"Oh, yeah, I have, too, but that doesn't mean I like it. What do you think, Jack? Have they got all the apples picked back home?"

The other McLaughlin, who was even less talkative than his brother, said, "They ought to."

Reuben strained to pick up his coffee cup, then wheezed out a long breath. "I'll tell ya, Homer, this time of year puts me in mind of a song you did last year. You know the one I'm talkin' about, don't you?"

"The one about Lonesome Jim?"

"Yeah, that's the one. I imagine you still know it, don't you?"

"Oh, I guess so."

"Well, some of these boys haven't heard it, and I'd like to hear it again."

Homer looked around at Ed and at the McLaughlins. "I don't have a mandolin or guitar or anything, so it's not much of a song. But I can do it if you don't mind."

"Go ahead," said Jory. Most of the songs we hear are that way anyway."

Ed nodded. "Sure. Let's hear it."

Homer looked at the McLaughlins, who said, "Oh, yeah, oh, yeah," like an echo.

The chair squeaked as Homer pushed it back and stood up. He blinked a couple of times, and the pale blue eyes had a faraway look until they came back to the little group in the bunkhouse.

"I made this up a few years back," he began. "Whenever I sing it, someone wants to know if it's a 'true story,' so I'll just say it's as true as any of the others I might tell you." Then in a clear, steady voice he sang.

Sometimes he rides in on a sorrel,
Sometimes he shows up on a bay.
He drifts from one ranch to another
In wintertime when there's no pay.

He does any chore that the ranch cook
Or foreman will ask him to do—
Sort beans, fetch the water and firewood,
Or cut up some spuds for the stew.

He keeps to his bunk in the evening,
You won't hear him brag or complain,
Till one morning his bedroll has vanished,
And he's off on the grubline again.

To folks who don't know him he's a drifter
Who goes here and there on a whim,
But out on the range we don't judge him,
This fella we call Lonesome Jim.

John D. Nesbitt

Come springtime he rides for an outfit
And works for a dollar a day,
Rides outlaws and ropes like a top hand
And never has too much to say.

Then roundup is done, and this loner
Gets off of his stake rope a while,
Cuts loose like a wolf on a full moon,
Sings Mexican songs with a smile.

He tells of the woman who left him,
And a woman who died in the snow—
And he hopes he can find him another
Who'll stay for the end of the show.

To folks who don't know him he's sorry,
A drunk from his spurs to his brim,
But out on the range we don't judge him,
This fella we call Lonesome Jim.

He drinks himself broke in November
Then lays up to get himself dry,
Goes back on the grubline for winter
With hopes that his hopes will not die.

We know him without ever knowing him,
We've seen it in others as well,
A man with a weakness that sometimes
He cannot control or dispell.

There's plenty of others who have it,
A weakness we're hard put to name—
It's not just for women or whiskey,
But it lives in the blood all the same.

To folks who don't know him he's a pity,
He'll never get straight or fit in,
But out on the range we don't judge him,
This fella we call Lonesome Jim.

No, out on the range we don't judge him,
We wish all the best luck to him—
For our own stories aren't all that different
From this fella we call Lonesome Jim.

    A round of applause came from the little bunkhouse audience, and Homer sat down.
    Ed had finished oiling his six-shooter and took more interest now. "Do you have many songs like that?" he asked.
    "Oh, a few. I haven't made up a new one for a while."
    "Good time of year comin' up for it," said Reuben.
    "Probably so. Maybe I'll make up one about Jory and the long-haired princess. Something with a happy ending."

* * * * *

    Ed appreciated his coat and gloves as he walked down the dim street. Homer was right. When the grey weather cleared out, a cold spell came in. On his way to town, Ed had noticed the chokecherry leaves turning red, the cottonwoods turning yellow. As soon as the sun went down, the air turned chilly, and he was glad to have a room where he could leave his gear and come back later to sleep.

He shivered, not just from the cold but from the anticipation of what he thought he might do. He had heard of this place when he worked at the blacksmith shop, but he had never dared to go there. Now he was putting himself up to it.

Down the street two blocks, he turned right on a street that was no better lit. In the middle of that block, he came to a building that stood by itself. Faint light showed behind the curtains of the only ground-floor window, and the front door was of solid wood. Still shivering, Ed took quick steps up onto the porch and knocked on the door. He could hear indistinct voices within, and thinking his knock might not have been loud enough, he took off his glove and tried again.

The door opened a hand's breadth, and a woman's eyes looked out. "What do you want?"

"I've heard there's girls here."

"Where are you from?"

"I just came in from a ranch, but I used to live here in town."

The woman opened the door and let him in. As he walked past her into the low-lit parlor, he saw that she was a busty woman, older, and in a full dress.

"You want to meet girls?" she said. "I have the best, as you can see for yourself." With her arm she directed his attention to a divan where three women sat, all smiling.

He gave the madam a questioning look.

"Go ahead, talk to them. Decide which one you like best, and ask her."

His heart was thumping, and he didn't know if he could speak. He took a deep breath as he looked at the first one, who had mouse-colored hair and a muddy complexion. His eyes roved and settled on the middle woman, older than he had in mind but soft and smiling, with straw-colored hair and blue eyes.

"What's your name?" he asked. His mouth was dry, and he was glad to find the words.

"Amelia. What's yours?"

"Ed."

She stood up and gave him her hand, and her low-cut dress offered him an inspiring view of her bosom. The desire welled up in him.

"You look like a gentleman, Ed. Do you like to go to the room?"

It was too quick to go back, even if he had wanted to. "Sure," he said, his mouth still dry.

She led him by the hand past the third woman, whom he did not even see, and down a hallway. She stopped at a door, turned the brass knob, led him into a room lit by one candle, and closed the door. As she raised both hands and opened his coat collar, she said, "I need the two dollars first."

"Oh, all right. I didn't know." He dug into his pocket.

"That's fine." She took the two silver dollars and set them on top of a high dresser. Then she went back to fiddling with his coat, undoing the top button. "Tell me what you like, Ed."

"Well, you know—"

"You like what all the boys like. I know." She moved down to the next button.

"Actually, this is the first time I ever—"

Her voice was soft as she slipped her hand inside his coat and rubbed his shirt. "That's all right, honey. Everyone has to have a first time."

"I'm afraid I'm goin' to do something wrong."

"Oh, no. Don't be afraid. You can't do anything wrong in here. Not with me. I know what's just right for a nice boy like you."

* * * * *

Back in his rented room, the lamplight seemed bright by comparison. As he reviewed the various parts of the interlude, he was satisfied. It was all done now, in another place, but it was real. Now he was on his own, here in Glenrose where he had started. As he looked over his gear, he thought he had made good use of his summer wages—a used saddle but a good one, a rope tied on to the right side, a rifle and scabbard on the left, a gunbelt looped on the saddle horn, and a pair of spurs hanging by their straps. It was a good feeling to have everything together. He could go from here. He figured he had enough to buy a horse—that, and pay his own way for a while as he went on to the next thing he had in mind.

Chapter Five

A light, dry snow was falling as Ed rode the buckskin down the main street of Litch. The town didn't look much different than it did five months before, and if anything, the weathered buildings and sparse plant life seemed to fit the harsh season better than the spring time.

Ed turned north on the cross street, rode a block and a half, and stopped in front of the Iris. The sign hadn't been touched up in the good part of the year, and from the buckling texture of the paint, the sign looked as if it might acquire more of a hieroglyphic aspect through the winter ahead.

Inside, Mrs. Porter cast her appraising eye on him. "Yes, sir?"

"I'd like to see about a room for the month."

Her eyes narrowed upon him. "Have you stayed here before?"

"Yes, I stayed two separate nights back in May. I shared a room both times with the same man. I believe you called him Mr. Shepard."

"I see. Well, there are more rooms to let at the present. Would you like one by yourself?"

"I wouldn't mind it."

"It's a little more, is all. Not double. The meals are the same, of course. You say you expect to stay a month."

"At least to begin with."

"That should be all right." She twisted her mouth, as if she were reluctant to mention money too directly, for fear of losing a boarder in the lean time of the year. "I'll need fifteen dollars for the first month. That covers room, meals, bath once a week, and laundry."

"My clothes?"

"Yes, within reason."

"How much would it be if I shared a room?"

"Twelve."

"A room to myself would be fine." He laid a ten-dollar gold piece and a five on the counter.

"Very well." She opened the registry book and turned it around to him. "If you could sign here, please." She lifted the two coins without a sound as he dipped the pen in the ink bottle. Before he had finished signing, her voice came out, higher now and almost cross. "You're the blacksmith boy."

"I was. For the last six months I've been doin' ranch work."

"And now that you're out of work, you come here."

"My money's good." He felt his resentment rising, and he realized he had been too sharp. Turning the register back to her, he took on a calmer tone and said, "I've minded my money all right, and I can get through the winter. My idea right now is to look around and see if there's an opportunity."

"That's your business," she said, a little smoothed out. "And as far as that goes, if you have anything you'd like to put in a safe, I have that as well." When he didn't answer, she pushed a key toward him. "You'll be next door to Mr. Shepard."

"Thank you." He took the key and went out to fetch his belongings.

* * * * *

During supper, he kept his eye out for Ravenna, who didn't appear until it was time to clear away the dishes. When she saw him, she did not show surprise, so he imagined Mrs. Porter had cautioned her. For his part, his pulse quickened each time she came into the room. She looked the same as before, her hair perhaps a little longer, but there was no aura about her to suggest that her situation had changed.

After the meal, he went to his room. Although he wanted nothing more than he wanted to get Ravenna off to one side and find out more about her circumstances, he knew he should not seem too impatient. He remembered Jory's comment about the steam engine, and he told himself he had plenty of time ahead of him.

Alone in his room, he pulled off his boots and stretched out to rest after the day's ride. He covered himself with his wool coat and stared at the ceiling. Before long, however, he began feeling restless. The sounds of Mr. Shepard coughing and clearing his throat came through the wall. Ed kept his arms crossed on his chest beneath the coat and tried to relax, but he felt like flinging the coat away, jumping to his feet, and slamming his fist into the wall. The guttural, hawking sound kept up. It was going to be a long winter.

After less than an hour of trying to relax, Ed sat up, swung his feet around, and pulled on his boots. He needed to go out and see what went on in this town after dark.

Two doors down from the livery stable where he had left his horse, he found an establishment called the Rimfire Saloon. The place was empty except for the bartender, so Ed took a spot at the bar and ordered a glass of whiskey. It would take him a while, as the taste of liquor did not appeal to him very much. The bartender, a red-headed man with a coarse complexion and swollen, spotty hands, poured the drink and went back to his stool beneath an overhead lamp, where he was etching something into a dark piece of leather about a foot square.

Ed stood with his elbow on the bar and took in a view of the place. It was a common-looking saloon, with deer antlers on two walls, a dusty stuffed bobcat up on a shelf behind the bar, and a five-foot set of Texas longhorns over the door. On a sideboard behind the bar sat a two-quart jar with a mound of rattlesnake buttons in the bottom.

After a while, the front door opened, and an old man came in. He wore a high, tobacco-colored wool cap with no beak, and a long ulster of about the same color. Although he walked with a halting step and tapped the floor with his stick, he did not seem in danger of falling over. He headed for a table not far from the bar and took a seat facing Ed.

When they had exchanged nods, the old man said, "How go the wars?"

"All right, I guess."

"Snow let up."

"That it did. Not much of it, really."

"No, not much. But we know what time of year we're movin' into. Short days, long cold nights. Hear the crickets inside now."

The red-haired bartender appeared with a glass of whiskey. He set it in front of the old man, who nodded and waved him off as if to say he didn't need anything else. Ed turned away to look at his own drink and to keep from staring at the other patron.

The old man's voice came up from his place at the table. "From here, or holed up for the night?"

Ed shifted to face him. "Just came to town. Think I might stay a while."

"There's worse places. Better ones, too." The man lifted his glass and took a drink, moved his lips outward and back, and let out a satisfied "Ahhh." He hunched his shoulders up and gave a tense shake. "That's the good stuff," he said. "Does what the hearth fire can't."

He opened his overcoat and took off his cap. He had straggling hair, mostly grey and with just a few wisps on top. Under thick eyebrows he had brown eyes with yellowish whites, and his lower face had a scattering of grey stubble. He blinked a couple of times, yawned, rubbed the corners of his eyes with both hands, reached inside his coat, and brought out a pair of spectacles which he put on. After a long sniff, he took another drink of whiskey.

"What do you do for work?" he asked.

"I just finished six months on a ranch. Season ended, of course."

"Oh, yeah. It's not a big item, right now. Ranch work."

"So I thought I'd look around for a while, see if anything comes up."

"No harm—oh, well, I guess there could be." The old man reached into his coat pocket and produced a gnarly, dark brown pipe with a long straight stem. With his other hand, he came up with a leather tobacco pouch. Looking down his nose, he stuffed the pipe and lit it. A cloud of smoke hung in front of his face and began to disperse. The old man swiped at the smoke to clear it away, then wrinkled his nose and spoke. "Who were you ridin' for, if you don't mind my askin'?"

"Cal Tompkins, out east and north of here."

"Oh, uh-huh. Who's his foreman now?"

"I don't know that he has a foreman as such, seein' as he does most of the bossin' himself, but Homer Dugdale is his right-hand man."

"Homer. Sure. You got along with him, I imagine."

"Everyone does."

The old man sucked on his pipe, then palmed the bowl and drew on it some more until he put out a solid puff of smoke. "You can sit here at the table if you want," he said. "There's room."

"Thanks. I think I will." Ed picked up his drink and carried it to the table. He took a seat at the old man's left, partly to make the speaking and listening easier and partly to be able to keep an eye on the bar and the front door.

"My name's Flood," said the old man. "Tyrel Flood."

"Pleased to meet you, Mr. Flood. I'm—"

"No need to mister me. Just call me Tyrel. And what did you say your name is?"

"I didn't, yet. It's Edward. Edward Dawes."

"Edward, eh? I think I knew your father."

Ed flinched. "Really?"

"The Prince of Wales. Ha-ha-ha."

"I don't know him."

"Neither do I, not personally. But there's been lots of Edwards, including the Black Prince. All just a joke, you know."

"Oh, sure. No harm." Ed watched as Tyrel frowned at his pipe and pulled another cloud of smoke out of it. "As far as that goes, you can just call me Ed."

"You'd think one name's as good as another."

"I guess so. I haven't thought about it."

"Well, if you do, you'll see it's not true."

Ed raised his eyebrows but said nothing.

"For one thing, you need to hang on to the same name. Once they take to callin' you Ed, you'd best not change to Hank, then to Oliver, and so on. So for you, once your name's Ed, it's better than any other one at random."

"I follow you."

"And as far as namin' someone to begin with, they're not all the same, either. Maybe there's not a big difference between Edward and Theodore, as they can both end up as Ted, but even at that, they wouldn't be any good for a girl. Furthermore, as far as boys' names go, Henry or Andrew are just better names than something like Dode or Dupe, and yet I've known fellas with those names."

"I suppose."

"That's why, when they get a good name for a king, they hang onto it, like Looie or Henry or Edward. So you see, you've got one of the best names in the world. Now me, for example, it would have been a hell of a lot easier if they'd called me Tyler, especially since he was president at the time, but Tyrel was an old family name. And even at that, it's better than Axel, which some men have for a name. To my ear, if your name's Axel, you lived a thousand years ago and burned down one another's wood castles."

"You've got it all worked out."

"Still, Axel's better than Dode. If my folks had named me Dode, I'd be sweepin' up in a train station somewhere."

"How about last names?"

"People don't pick those, unless they've got a good reason, like a personal history they'd like to get rid of, or the name doesn't sound good in English. For example, you come from Germany and your name's Snotter, maybe you change it."

"Something like Snyder."

"That's right. Or maybe you go into a grog shop and come out happy with the name of Mead, or you go into a vintner's and come out rosy-cheeked and calling yourself Portwine." Tyrel started laughing, then laughed some more, and seemed unable to stop. At last he settled down and said, "I'm sorry. I know what it's like to have to listen to someone laugh at his own jokes." He took off his spectacles and wiped his eyes. "I do it all the time." He went into another laugh, shorter this time, and then pulled himself out of it and took a drink from his whiskey.

Ed, meanwhile, said nothing. He found it amusing, but not quite enough to laugh at.

Tyrel wrinkled his nose. "So tell me about yourself." He lifted the tip of his index finger, which had a yellow, ridged fingernail that looked as thick and hard as horn, and dug into the bowl of his pipe.

Ed pursed his lips, thought for a second, and began. "Not much to tell. I was orphaned early on, got adopted and grew up on a farm, went to work in a blacksmith shop for a year, then tried my hand at cow-punchin', which I already told you about."

"No wonder you jumped when I said I knew your father."

"Did I jump?"

"Not very high. But that's the way it goes. Very few people know when to keep their mouths shut, especially around strangers."

"Isn't that the truth?"

Tyrel paused from digging in his pipe. "Sure. It's like the fella who's waitin' for a streetcar. Another man comes up and asks, 'D-do you kn-know what t-time it is?' The fella is wearin' a watch, but he points with his thumb to the fella standin' next to him. So the stranger says again, 'D-do you kn-know what t-time it is?' 'Sure,' the other one says. He takes out his watch and tells him, 'It's half past two.' The stranger says, 'Th-thanks,' and walks away. Then the man who told him the time says to the first fella, 'Hey, what's the matter with you? You're wearin' a watch just like I am. Why wouldn't you give him the time?' So the first person says, 'D-did you w-want m-me to g-get a k-kick in the ass?'"

Ed laughed along with the old man this time. "That was all right," he said. "It had a good surprise."

"I guess so. Some people look for the lesson, like somethin' about talkin' to strangers. But really, there isn't any, not if you consider the fella that asks the first question." Tyrel turned his pipe over and rapped it on the table top, and a small pile of black grains spilled out. "There's another one, about a fella in Mexico who wants to buy two tickets to Culiacán, but it's in Spanish and it doesn't translate worth a damn."

"Oh."

"And it has to be acted out. Thrust of the hips. Play on words with *culo* and *culi*. Funny as hell, though."

"I bet."

"It's all funny."

"Everything?"

"If you want it to be. At this point." He went about putting tobacco in his pipe again. "How about you? You don't talk much."

"I already told my life story."

"Such as it was. I'm not one to pry, though."

"I don't have the gift of gab."

"I suppose I do. Leastwise, I don't like to drink alone." Tyrel poked at the tobacco with his crusty fingertip. "So you finished cowpunchin' for the year, and you're lookin' around."

"That's about it."

The old man struck a match, and it sputtered into flame. "Well, I been around these parts for quite a while, so if there's anything I can tell you, let me know. Be glad to help." He laid the match over the bowl of the pipe and started puffing.

"There might be one thing."

"Oh?"

"Have you noticed that some anthills are peaked and made of tiny grains of sand and rock, while others are mounded up and have bits of grass and twigs and pine needles and such?"

Tyrel raised his thick eyebrows above the rim of his spectacles, then lowered them. "Now that you mention it, yes."

"Why do you think that is?"

"I don't know. I'd say ants are like people. Different ones have different ways of doin' things. I know that's not very scientific. I *have* thought it would be interesting to take a shovel and dig down into one or two of them anthills, but then I think, why not leave 'em alone?

They're just tryin' to make a livin' like everyone else." He drew out a rich cloud of smoke. "That's not scientific, either. It's more philosophical."

"How about snakes?"

"Oh, that's different. You've got to kill them, poisonous ones anyway, before they do somethin' to you."

"Or after."

"That's for damn sure." Tyrel took a drink from his whiskey glass. "Snakes are all gone down into their holes for the winter. Now, they say that's somethin' interestin' to dig into, is a rattlesnake den. Catch 'em while they're still hibernatin', shovel 'em out like pieces of rope, and finish 'em off. Cut their heads off, or throw 'em in a fire."

Ed glanced at the two-quart jar. "Some folks collect the rattles."

"They can have 'em." A puff on the pipe. "I'll tell you a story about why I don't like snakes. This happened more'n twenty years ago, when I first came out here. We were buildin' a station on the old trail near La Bonte Creek—I was a carpenter before my knee went bad—and we were camped next to the job. One mornin' I woke up, and there was a stinkin' rattlesnake coiled up in the cast-iron skillet, not six feet from my head. I'll tell you, I cut his head off with a shovel and scrubbed that skillet a dozen times with sand. Seemed like I couldn't get the smell out of the pan, but I think I had it in my nose and kept smellin' it that way."

"Like a skunk."

"Somethin' like that. But a snake smell is more sickenin'." Tyrel drank the last of his whiskey. He looked at Ed's glass, which hadn't gone down much. He seemed to be weighing his options.

Ed spoke. "I'll be glad to buy you a drink."

Tyrel paused with his mouth open, and Ed saw the man's narrow, tapering, yellow teeth, spaced at the tips and with gaps where a couple were gone. "Nah," said the old man, "I usually have only one drink in here."

"I'll pay for this one."

"Not necessary. He's already put it on my bill. But I thank you." Tyrel gathered up his pouch and put his cap on his head, then stuck his pipe in his mouth and pushed himself up with his stick. "If you're gonna be in town a while and need to kill some time, come by my place. I live on the next street north, last house on the right as you go west. We'll drink cheaper there."

"I might do that. What's the bartender's name, anyway?"

"Dode."

"Really?"

Tyrel laughed as he held his pipe with his teeth. "Nah, you call him that, and he'll think you're callin' him Toad. His name's Henry." With a half-smile on his face, the old man turned and walked away, tapping his stick as he went.

* * * * *

After a couple of days, Ed formed an idea of Ravenna's schedule. She worked through the morning and noon meals, then had a little time off from two to about four, when she went to work on the evening meal. On the third day, when he saw Mrs. Porter getting wrapped up to go out, he lingered in the sitting room. When the landlady had gone down the steps, he went into the dining room. Ravenna was straightening the chairs on the other side of the table.

"Oh," she said, looking up.

He smiled. "Why don't you sit down for a few minutes?"

"I shouldn't, really."

"Don't you usually get a little time to yourself in the afternoon? Seems to me you do, and you deserve it."

She wavered with her hand on the back of a chair.

He ventured to say, "Ever since that day last spring when we talked for a few minutes, I've thought we've had something in common."

Her dark eyes softened. "It seemed like it. But every man and boy who comes through here wants me to listen to his story."

"Even Mr. Shepard?"

"Well, no."

"Maybe you see me like the rest, but I hope not. After all, you do know me a little bit, and I'm going to be here for a while, so it's not as if I'm a complete stranger."

"I know."

He gave what he hoped was an encouraging look. "Well, sit down here for a few minutes. There's no harm. It's all in the open."

She shrugged, and with a smile that seemed apologetic, she pulled out a chair and sat down. "Mrs. Porter says you quit being a blacksmith's boy and went to work being a cow-boy."

"I suppose I did. But I was free to do what I wanted. I wasn't indentured. Are you?"

"No. I don't know if anybody is, these days."

"Don't you think it's all right, then, if a person wants to make a change?"

"For you, I suppose." She looked around and lowered her voice a little. "But it's different for a girl."

"But you know what I mean?"

"Oh, yes."

"I thought you would understand."

Her eyes brightened, and her smile was relaxed. "So are you planning to keep on doing the same thing?"

"You mean ranch work? I think so, at least for another year or two. How about yourself?"

She made a light puff with her lips. "I'm not at a point where I have a plan. So far, I just work one day to the next, one month to the next."

"There's nothing wrong with that."

"I guess not. It's hard for a girl to have a plan anyway. Everyone expects she'll have someone else to make decisions for her."

"Seems like it."

"And how about you? After you've been a cow-boy for a couple of years, what do you want to do next?"

He looked at her soft, clear features. Here was a person like himself, who came from nowhere. He wondered if she thought the same way he did—if she wondered how much a person could hope for or expect, how much a person had a right to want something. "To tell you the truth," he said, "I don't have it laid out ahead of me. But there's something I have to do before I do anything else."

Her eyes showed interest. "What's that?"

Now it was his turn to look around. "I haven't told this to anyone else, and I probably won't until I have to."

She nodded.

"But you remember what I told you about the first part of my growing up? I said I lived with my grandfather, and he died. Well, I don't know for sure if he was my grandfather. I called him Pa-Pa, and he was like a father to me. But the people who took me in told me he was my grandfather, so that's the way I left it."

She leaned forward. "And you want to find out?"

"That's part of it. The other part is, he didn't just die."

Her facial expression widened.

"Someone came and killed him, and as far as I know, no one was called to answer for it. But I have an idea who it was."

Ravenna did not act girlish as he thought she might. She just looked at him and nodded.

"What I want to do is find out why—who was behind it if someone was, and why that person would want to kill this man who cared for me like a father." He let out a long breath. "After that, I can decide what to do next. But until then, this is the thing I have to do."

She moved her head up and down in a slow motion. "You have to do it for the man who cared for you as well as for yourself. And because it's just not right."

"That's it. That's the whole thing."

* * * * *

Shortly after he went to his room, Ed heard Mrs. Porter come in. The house went quiet again. No sounds came from the room next door nor from any of the other lodgers, most of whom Ed imagined were at their day's work. Figuring he had a good three hours before he even thought of getting ready for supper, he put on his hat and coat and went out for a walk.

He had checked on the horse in the morning, so he didn't need to go there. Nor did he want to go to a saloon this early, though he realized that any time of day might be suitable for his purposes. In the few days he had spent in town so far, he had walked up and down all of the streets. He knew where Tyrel Flood's house, or shack, was located, and he decided to drop by there for a visit.

The shack was built of dark lumber—vertical boards and battens—and had a small, slanted porch with an overhead covering. Ed stepped up from the dirt path onto the porch and knocked on the door.

"Come in!" came the call.

Ed turned the knob and pushed the door inward.

"Come in," said the old man again.

Ed crossed the threshold and squinted in the dark interior, where the only light came through the front window. He made out Tyrel Flood sitting in a wooden armchair and wearing his cap and overcoat.

"Hello, there," said the old man. "I believe you two know each other." He waved his hand to the right, where Mr. Shepard sat in a stuffed chair.

As Ed nodded to both men, he observed a whiskey bottle sitting on a low table between them.

"Sit down, sit down." Tyrel pointed at a straight-backed chair next to the window. "Wait. Get yourself a glass first, and I won't have to get up."

Ed went through an open doorway to a kitchen area, where dirty dishes were stacked on a sideboard. A mottled brown-and-yellow cat rose up from the mess, dropped to the floor, and glided into a bedroom. Ed opened a cupboard and found a glass. Back in the living room, he poured himself two fingers of whiskey and took a seat by the dirty window.

"Cam was tellin' me earlier that you have an interest in the King Diamond ranch."

"Not much."

"Says you asked about old Snake Eyes."

"That was a while back."

Tyrel laughed. "Nothin' wrong with bein' careful, like we said the other night. But unless I miss my guess, I'd say you're not cut from the same cloth as them fellers."

"I don't know them."

"Suffice it to say that Cam used to, but he was a little too honest for them. Isn't that right, Cam?"

Ed looked at Mr. Shepard, who nodded as he sat with his eyes half-closed and seemed to be melting into his armchair.

Tyrel raised his glass and drank from it. "You're among friends here, boy, if you want to be. Whatever your interest is in the King Diamond Ranch is your business, but if there's anything I can tell you about Snake Eyes or his boss, old Ramses, don't be too shy to ask."

Ed took a sip of his whiskey. "I suppose there might be one thing."

"And what would that be?"

"Why do you call him Ramses?"

Tyrel laughed. "Oh, that's just a joke. Ramses was a big shot in ancient Egypt. One of the pharaohs. This fella acts like that, so we've got our little joke."

"I see."

"There's a little joke in everything, don't you think?"

"Most things, maybe."

"Well, don't worry, anyway. Talkin' like this is just a way to pass the time." Tyrel held his glass up in salute, and Ed did the same. Over in the stuffed chair, Cam Shepard hoisted his in a slow, uncertain motion.

Chapter Six

Ravenna came down the steps in a long wool coat and a fur cap. The coat, which had the darkness of her hair but not the glossy texture, stood out in contrast with the snow in the background. Her cheeks had good, rosy color, and her eyes were lively as she smiled.

"Mrs. Porter thinks you're a wonderful young man for clearing the snow this way."

Ed tossed a shovelful aside into the street. "Don't mind it at all. It's good exercise, makes me feel better after being inside so much. And it doesn't cost me anything."

"It would cost her something. It did last year, she said, but she didn't tell me how much."

Ed worked on, enjoying the exertion and appreciating the attention. "Doesn't matter."

"Mr. Shepard told her you clean off old Mr. Flood's doorstep and walkway as well."

"It's not as much as here. It's somethin' to do, and it's a lot easier for me than it would be for him." Ed looked at the steps he had just cleared, and he was glad Ravenna had been the first person to walk on them. "Did she say anything about it?"

"Not really. I don't think she cares for him, though."

Ed gave a short laugh. "I wouldn't expect her to."

Ravenna stepped onto the sidewalk to keep up with him as he moved along. "She says you could be charging."

"Him, not her."

She laughed. "I think so. But other places as well."

He spoke across his shoulder as he turned to toss the snow. "It would be a slow way to make anything." He paused and rested the shovel. "Whatever there is to be made, I wouldn't want to be takin' it from the boys in town. Just doin' this little bit, I'm causin' someone a loss of income."

"But not by doing Mr. Flood's."

"Probably not. I think if I didn't do it, it wouldn't get done very often. The snow would just get trampled, like it does elsewhere, and that's no good for an old man who gets around like he does." Ed shoveled until he went past the edge of Mrs. Porter's property, then straightened up and turned to meet Ravenna's cheerful face.

"It's kind of you to think of others," she said.

He smiled as if he had been caught at mischief. "It's easy to do right now. I don't have anything else pressing me. But don't think I'm too much of an angel."

Her eyes were roving over his features, searching. "I know. Nobody is. Especially when things have been done to you."

He felt that she went right into him. "You're prettiest when you get serious."

Her eyes still played over him. "You know what I mean."

"I do. It makes you different. You lose something. That's why it seems like you and I found each other. We're alike in that way."

She lingered for a moment and nodded. Then she stepped back and turned. "Well, now that you're finished here, what will you do next? Go do Mr. Flood's?"

"I think so. Then I'll check on my horse."

"Mrs. Porter says a horse is an expense."

"It is, but I saved money buying this one when I did. The price of horses goes down when you're goin' into winter because you're lookin' at feedin' 'em. Unless, of course, you just pull their shoes and turn 'em out to graze for themselves."

"So you saved the money that you'll spend keeping him for the winter?"

"Something like that. And furthermore, it's worth it to me to have a horse on hand if I need it."

She came to the steps and paused. "I wish you would bring him by some day and show him to me. I'd like to see him."

"I'll do that. I usually take him out the other way, but I'll bring him by here."

He watched as she turned and went up the steps. *I'm going to kiss you some day*, he thought.

* * * * *

With three recent snowstorms less than a week apart, the snow had piled up on the rangeland as well as in town. In the Rimfire Saloon, Ed heard that the deer from the breaks north of town had come down onto the flats, and some of the men from town had knocked off half a dozen. Meat was meat, the talk went. Keep 'em off the haystacks.

Ed brought the buckskin to the rail in front of the boarding house, and when he went in for his rifle, he invited Ravenna to come out and see the horse.

"Oh, he's nice-looking," she said. "I like the dark mane and the light color on the rest of him. Almost like a palomino, isn't it?"

"That's why they call it a buckskin. Color of tanned deerhide. If he's got a cream-colored mane and tail, they call him a palomino, and if he's got a black mane and tail, he's a buckskin."

"I like him. No wonder you bought him." She turned her eyes from the horse to the rifle and scabbard Ed held at his side. "So you're going to go get a deer."

"Going to try."

"What will you do with it?"

"If I get one, I'll give it to Mrs. Porter. Clean it first, of course. Maybe give a little of it to Tyrel Flood." He shrugged. "It's somethin' to do, anyway."

"Well, good luck."

"Thanks. If I'm not back by dark, take it as a good sign. If I'm back earlier, you can guess I didn't do any good."

He tied on the scabbard so it rode under his left leg with the rifle stock forward. With his rope tied on the other side, he was ready to go, so he swung aboard and rode north out of town.

From the talk in the Rimfire Saloon, a man would think that all he had to do was ride a ways out of town, shoot a deer by the side of the road, and come back. It became evident, however, that things weren't going to be that easy. The deer, if there were any left that hadn't been run off, were not standing around in plain sight.

Ed rode for a couple of miles through a white expanse. He saw horse tracks coming and going but no signs of a hunting party or big slaughter. The wind had blown since the day before, so he imagined all the earlier marks had been covered over. He kept an eye out for fresh deer tracks. After a while, he saw a set that crossed the road and led off into a small draw to his left. A winding row of leafless bushes and low trees showed what was most likely a watercourse in good weather and a bit of shelter in times like this.

Dropping off the road, he followed the tracks for a quarter of a mile and decided to dismount. Lifting one boot at a time out of the snow, he took off his spurs and put them in the near saddlebag. He pulled out the rifle and went ahead on foot, leading the horse.

In his field of vision, there were only two colors—the dazzling white of the full cover of snow, and the greyish-brown branches that stuck up here and formed shadowy nooks there. What a hunter did was look for shapes out of place.

After half an hour of trudging, he saw such a shape. First he saw the ears and nose, then the husky front quarters and straight back until the hindquarters disappeared behind a screen of snow-laden branches.

He crouched in front of the horse, hoping that most of his shape would be absorbed by the larger form in back of him. The deer was stock-still, its head against a background of branches. Then the head turned, and two branches turned with it.

Ed levered in a shell, slow and quiet, and brought up the rifle. The rear sight came into view, lined up with the bead of the front sight, and found the dark center of the deer's front quarters. When everything came together, Ed fired.

The deer lurched, leaping up and out from the cover. It took two bounds, floundered backwards, and fell over.

Meanwhile, the buckskin was pulling back on the reins. Ed held on tight, facing the horse and pulling straight back and down. When he had the animal settled down, he tried poking the rifle into the scabbard, but the horse kept moving away. After a long minute of resistance, Ed got the rifle put away and led the buckskin forward.

After a hundred and fifty yards of slogging through the snow, he felt a quick lift at seeing bright specks of blood on the white blanket. A few yards beyond, he saw an antler, motionless, sticking out of the snow where the deer fell. Now the work would begin.

He used the rope to tie his horse to the bushes, not wanting to have the buckskin pull away and run off, leaving him out here on foot with a dead deer. From the right saddlebag, he took out a leather sheath holding a bone-handled knife. He put it on his belt. Next he stamped and shuffled until he had a six-foot area packed down well enough to work on. Pulling the deer by its antlers, he dragged it into the open space and took a breather to look at it. The buck was admirable, with three tines on each side plus eye guards, and it laid out as a big animal. It had a dark chest, a tan-grey coat, and a creamy underside. There would be meat for a while.

After an hour of stooping and straining, he had the deer field-dressed and the cavity drained. He washed his hands in the snow, cleaned his knife, and went for the horse. After putting the sheath knife back in the saddlebag, he untied the buckskin and led him up to the deer so the horse could see it and smell it.

Doubting his own ability to wrestle the floppy carcass up onto the saddle of a sashaying horse, Ed trussed the deer's front feet against its neck and snugged the rope around the base of the antlers. All this time, he had the other end of the rope tied to the horse's neck. Now he untied it, led the horse around by the reins to face the deer, held the loose end of the rope on the off side of the saddle, and mounted up. As soon as he did, he remembered his spurs in the saddlebag, but once the horse leaned into pulling the weight, Ed decided to wait and see how things would go. He wrapped the rope around the saddle horn and nudged the horse with his heel.

The cover of snow, a foot deep on the average, made for smooth dragging. The carcass slid along, jerking once in a while but not hanging up.

When Ed came to the road, he stopped the horse for a breather. He gazed up the trail to his left, and the appearance of a dark figure sent a jolt to the pit of his stomach. A horse and rider had just come out of the breaks a half-mile away. Even at the distance, Ed knew as if by instinct that the man was the old assassin Bridge.

A second rider came out of the breaks, a heavier man on a taller horse. He caught up with the first rider and fell in alongside.

If it were anyone else in the world, Ed might have asked for help in getting the deer up and onto the horse, but he knew he did not want to talk to these two men right now. He did not want them to know him yet. He wanted to meet them at a time of his choosing.

He knew they had seen him, though, and even if there had been cover for him to duck into, doing so would make him look suspicious. As it was, he was just someone with meat on the ground.

Staying off the road and a foot or so below it on the slope, he turned the buckskin toward town, pulled the deer into plain view, and dismounted. He checked over the rigging on his horse, and then, in no hurry, he took his spurs from the saddlebag and buckled them on, first the left and then the right. When he was still bent over, he heard the riders approaching.

They had put their horses into a lope, and the hooves were drumming. Closer now, then even, then past him they rode, with leather creaking and bits jingling. Ed stood up, close to the left shoulder of the buckskin. He saw enough of Bridge to confirm what he already knew, and he caught only the hind view of the blocky man in the large hat. That was fine with Ed. He would get a good look at both of these jaspers, more than once, as time went on. He pulled the glove onto his left hand and then, before pulling on the right glove, he flicked his middle fingernail against the stock of the rifle.

* * * * *

Even though it was a slow drag, Ed made it back to town with the deer before dark. After skinning and quartering it, he hung the meat on Mrs. Porter's back porch. The hide was pretty well worn and not worth saving, but he cut out the antlers and hung them on a rafter near the quarters of meat.

After supper, he decided it would be a good night to visit the Rim-fire Saloon. A few patrons were standing along the bar when he walked in, so he took a place next to a fur hunter he had met a week or so earlier. Ferguson, or Ferg, as he liked to be called, took interest in Ed's story about the deer. He asked for details about where Ed had left the gut-pile.

"That'll bring in coyotes," he said. "I bet we could go out there in the mornin' and get one or two."

"Probably could."

"Are you interested? I could set up a tripod, and you could pick 'em off at two, three hundred yards."

"Then you sell the pelts?"

"That's the idea. But to tell you the truth, I don't make that much on the hides. A little bit. I'm more in it for the shootin'."

"You like that part."

"Oh, yeah. You would, too. You get a good set-up, say a dead cow or this gut-pile of yours, and they come right in. And there's sportsmen that'll pay good money to do it." Ferg's eyes lit up. "I'm learnin' how to call 'em. That's when it really gets good. They come right at you, and you shoot 'em close."

Ed didn't have anything to say.

"These on the gut-pile, though, they'll be longer range. But it's still good sport, seein' how good a shot you can make, and watchin' that dog toss in the air when you hit 'em good." Ferg seemed to be waiting for an answer, and not getting one, he spoke again. "So what do you think? You wanta go out in the morning?"

Ed shook his head. "I don't think so. I can see how you like it, but I just don't see the fun in it for me."

Ferg nodded. "That's all right. But you can think about it, and if you want to try it later on, let me know."

All the time he was talking with Ferg, Ed kept an eye out along the length of the bar. A little over half-way down, he saw the two men he had seen earlier on the trail. As soon as he finished the conversation with Ferg, Ed shifted his position to get a better look at the other two.

Bridge did not seem to have changed a speck in the passage of several years. If the flat-brimmed, flat-crowned black hat was the not the same one as before, it was identical. Likewise appeared the dark overcoat, the black neckerchief, and the narrow black leather vest. Even more impressive to Ed were the facial features—the long, thin nose, the dark, beady, close-set eyes, and the thin lips—which had a timeless quality about them, as if the man had come into being at the age of thirty-five or forty and would stay there until he went out.

At the moment he smoked a narrow, tight cigarette, which stuck out of the corner of his thin mouth like a toothpick and bobbed up and down as he talked. The man did not smile, nor did he raise his voice or move his hands about, except now, when with thumb and forefinger he pinched the cigarette from the crook of his mouth and dropped it on the floor, followed by a faint twist of the body.

On the far side of Bridge, to his left, stood the other man Ed had seen that afternoon. He was half a head taller than Bridge and built on a bigger scale. He had a large hat and a broad vest, all in proportion to his meaty face and thick lips. Louder as well, he had a gravelly voice that carried even when the words didn't. Whereas Bridge stood up straight and did not touch the bar, this man leaned with his left hand on the polished wood. From time to time, he pushed back and spat toward the floor, where a spittoon would be.

Ed moved aside to let another man shoulder in and order a drink. Bridge and his partner went out of view. Ed stood in that arrangement for a couple of minutes, not liking the other man so close at his left elbow. He shifted again, then picked up his drink and stepped back from the bar.

Now he had a full view, and he only needed to form a few quick impressions without making himself too obvious. He took in Bridge's black holster and gunbelt with the dark-handled butt of a pistol sticking up. The other man had a deep-stained brown gunbelt and a six-gun with a walnut handle. Both men also wore their spurs.

As he let his gaze drift back up toward the bar, Ed saw something that took him by surprise. Bridge's partner had turned to speak to the man on his left, a broad-backed man in a sack coat who tipped back his hat and showed himself to be none other than Jeff, the puncher from Arkansas who had names for all the dominoes.

In no hurry to be recognized by Jeff or to be remembered by the other two, Ed moved back to an empty spot at the bar. He toyed with his drink a while longer, then tossed down the last of it and went home for the night.

* * * * *

Ravenna watched as Ed cut away a chunk of venison from the hanging hindquarter.

"It's generous of you to share your deer meat with Mr. Flood," she said.

"I figure there's enough to go around." The meat was firm and cold but not yet frozen, and as he hefted the piece and laid it on the brown paper, he guessed it to weigh about five pounds. "This should keep all right for a couple of days, make him and his cat both happy. I suppose it's been a while since he's been able to go out and get one for himself."

Ravenna nodded in approval at the clean cut of meat. "It's good to be able to do something like this, isn't it?"

"Do you mean to have the game available, or to have the ability to go after it?"

"Both, I guess, but I was thinking more of the latter. Some men, even out here where we don't have all the comforts, wouldn't want to get their hands soiled."

"I know what you mean. Finicky. But that's not a problem here. None of this bothers you, does it?"

"Oh, no. I don't care for killing chickens, because it's so messy, but as far as the idea, or the blood itself—no, I could do it if I had to."

"That's good." Ed folded the paper and wrapped the package. "You know, the Indian women have to do all the butcherin', when the men bring it in from the hunt."

Ravenna smiled. "I know, and they slaughter the puppies themselves. I don't know if I would go that far, swinging a stone hatchet."

"We'll hope we don't have to." He lifted the package and let it settle in his hand. "Well, I think I'll take this to him now. Um, this knife is Mrs. Porter's. I'll leave it in the kitchen on the way."

* * * * *

The old man was sitting in his arm chair and drinking coffee when he hollered for Ed to come in. "Well," he called out at the sight of the package, "what have you got there?"

"I found a deer yesterday when I didn't have anything better to do, and I thought I'd bring you some of it."

"Well, good for you." The old man looked around. "Just set it on the table here. Go get yourself a cup of coffee if you want. It's a little too early in the day to be drinkin' the stronger stuff. Hope you don't mind."

"Not at all." Ed went to the kitchen, found the coffee pot on the stove, and poured himself a cup. Back in the living room, he took a seat by the window as before. The room was chilly, so he did not take off his hat and coat. He noticed that Tyrel was wrapped up in his overcoat and cap as well.

"What did you bring me, some tough old hocks?"

"No, I brought a piece of hindquarter. You can slice it into steaks, or do whatever you want with it."

"Fry it in bacon grease, that's what. If I can keep Grimalkin here from getting to it first." He poked with his stick at the cat, which had come slinking into the room and held its head up at the edge of the table. "Get away, now." Tyrel rested the stick against his leg again. "What else?"

"Not much."

"Glad to know you got out and did somethin'. Hate to think of a brave young fella like yourself fritterin' away his time in a boarding house, even if there is good scenery." He waved his hand and said, in an aside, "Cam told me." Then in his normal tone, he asked, "Been to the saloon lately?"

"Went for a little while last night."

"I can't afford to go there very often, but I like to keep my hand in. Not that anyone cares, or would miss me if I dried up and blew away." Tyrel leaned forward and set his empty cup on the table. "Who was there?"

"I talked a little while with Ferguson, the fur hunter. He offered to take me out to shoot coyotes, but I didn't take him up on it."

"Bah. Probably didn't miss much. Any time you get around those things, you end up with fleas, ticks, or lice. Just dirty."

Ed found it noteworthy that someone as unkempt as Tyrel would make a disparaging comment about hygiene, but he imagined the old man had a sense of dignity in spite of his scruffy exterior.

After a few seconds, Tyrel spoke again. "They smell, too, these trappers do. I think it's hard to get that smell off. Hey, there." He nudged the cat with his stick. "I knew a coon hunter that had his cat flesh out his hides for him. Probably a good cat, but I bet he took to smellin' rank, too."

"Might have. Sometimes you get a whiff of Ferguson."

Tyrel brought out his pipe and rapped it upside-down in his palm, then flicked the debris on the floor. He blew through the stem, poked his little finger in the bowl, rapped again, and frowned. He leaned back and reached into his trousers pocket, from which he took a small clasp knife with a white handle like whalebone. He opened the blade and started scraping the bowl of the pipe.

It was Ed's turn to break the silence. "Saw a couple of other fellas in there last night, too."

"Oh?"

"That fella named Bridge. That's his name, isn't it?"

"Ol' Snake Eyes? Yeah."

"And he had another fella with him. Larger, heavier sort."

"That would be Cooley. They ride together."

"That fits. I saw 'em ride into town, and later I saw 'em in the saloon."

"Yeah, Bridge used to be more of a lone wolf, but since Cooley's been workin' there, you often see the two of 'em."

"How long's that been?"

"Oh, I don't know. A few years at least. Since Cam worked there, I'd say."

Ed put away the information and moved to the next bit. "Then I saw another fella I knew. Name of Jeff, comes from Arkansas. He worked at the same place I did last season."

"With Homer."

"Yep. He took off the minute he drew his wages, and this is the first time I've seen him since. He seemed to be striking up a conversation with this one you call Cooley. Maybe he knows him. Puncher named Jeff, a little on the stocky side but not as big as Cooley. Says he comes from Arkansas. Always has a smart rattle of talk."

Tyrel shook his head. "Doesn't sound familiar, but there's a lot of 'em come and go. Well, like you, as far as that goes."

Ed shrugged. "He didn't come into town with them, so I'd guess he was just makin' friends."

"Some friends. But that's up to him. Me, I stay clear of 'em."

*****

Ravenna stood by as Ed separated the dark, lean meat from the bone. He had finished the first hindquarter and was working on the second, his left hand bloody and his right hand wielding the kitchen knife.

"What's got you frowning?" she asked.

"Just somethin' I was thinkin' about."

"You look serious."

"I suppose I am." He let his eyes meet hers, and he felt as before that the two of them shared a view on things that did not have to be parsed out in full detail. He spoke in a lower voice. "You remember a while back when I told you I thought I knew the person who had done a bad thing?"

"Of course."

"Well, I saw that person again yesterday."

She took in a slow breath. "Are you sure?"

"Yes. I saw him twice, in the company of his saddle pard. No mistake about who he is or who he works for."

"They're here?"

Still in a lower voice, he said, "They come into town from a place out in Thunder Basin." He drew his eyebrows together and lowered his voice even further. "Have you ever heard anything about the King Diamond Ranch or a couple of men named Bridge and Cooley?"

Ravenna shook her head.

"Well, consider it as if I didn't mention it. But what I need to do, when the good weather comes, is get to know more about these fellas. I don't know if the man who did this thing was actin' on his own or if he was doin' it for some else. That means I have to find out if the owner of the ranch ever knew the man who, um, it happened to."

"Pa-Pa."

Her utterance was like magic, as if she had merged her being with his. Their eyes met in perfect understanding, and the lips that had spoken those two syllables were beautiful beyond everything. With his hands raised and apart so he would not touch her with his work, he leaned toward her and met her lips with his.

Chapter Seven

As Ed rode north to Thunder Basin, he felt the assurance that came with being well equipped. The buckskin had wintered well and now stepped out at a brisk pace. The saddle rode easy. Ed had oiled it so it was soft to the touch, and he had tipped it upside down and powdered the cracks to take out some of the squeaks. The rifle at his left knee and the rope at his right gave him a feeling of readiness, as did the six-gun riding on his hip.

The sun felt warm on his back, just as it did when he came this way a year earlier. The snow had melted, and green was coming up into the grassland again. The songs of the meadowlarks and the black-and-white birds resonated in the clear air, not yet dry from the morning dew.

The horse's hooves kept up a steady rhythm of *tlock-tlock, tlock-tlock*. Ed stayed balanced with the movement of the buckskin, feeling in harmony with the animal, drawing the slack on the reins every two or three minutes to keep the harmony neat.

He rode easy, not pushing the horse. As before, he had the sense of going into a vast interior country, a land unto itself, a long ride in from any of the main-traveled roads. In the core of that country were two men—as he pictured them, two worms in an apple. One he knew by sight and hated by heart, while the other was yet a faceless figure that moved in dim light. Ed was determined to get a better look at Mort Ramsey, learn what he could, and decide from there. As for Bridge, he had assumed long ago what he would do to that man if the right chance came around. He would just have to do it clean. Meanwhile, as long as he did not tip his hand, he was in no hurry.

In late afternoon he came to the valley of the dead cottonwoods. It looked unchanged from the year before—first the orange hills to the east with the lone dead pine on the ridge, then the tops of the bare trees visible for a mile as they reached out of the creek bottom, and then the lifeless colony of prairie dog holes with dead tumbleweeds for wreaths. Ed watered his horse and made his camp in the peace of evening.

In the morning he hit the trail early, moving through broken country and coming to the gateway of the King Diamond Ranch before the sun had risen very high. He paused a moment to take stock of himself and all his gear, to remember each thing in its place. An image of Ravenna passed through his mind, and he felt the strength of her encouragement. He squared his shoulders and sat up straight. Raising his head, he cast his view outward, sweeping the hazy buttes that lay at a day's ride in every direction. Then he gathered his reins, touched his spurs to the buckskin, and followed the trail as it wound through horse-high brush toward the headquarters of the ranch.

The trail kept to higher ground, curving to the north and coming around south to the ranch buildings. A quarter-mile before he reached the headquarters, Ed paused to observe the layout, which from this angle looked a little different than it did from the main road. Situated on a bench above a drainage or bowl, the buildings lay along a curve, following the contour of the land. A rider approaching, then, could see the front of each building, just as, Ed imagined, a person in front of any of those buildings could see company when it came calling.

First in line lay a plain structure of weathered lumber. It had all the appearances of a bunkhouse, with a hitch rack, a front door, a stovepipe, and an outhouse. After the bunkhouse there loomed a taller, broader building made of logs. As with the gateway, Ed imagined the logs had been hauled a long distance, and he could see that a great deal of labor had gone into the construction of the lodge-like ranch house. Instead of having a plain gabled roof with two straight runs, the house had an asymmetrical distribution of gables and dormer windows. On the main level, a covered porch with slender log railings stretched across the front of the house, with thick plank steps leading up.

Beyond the oddly matched living quarters, which Ed guessed had been built by two separate owners, stood a plain, normal-looking barn that had its doors closed. On the other side of the barn sat a lower building that looked like a wagon or equipment shed. The dry, hard-packed ranch yard widened out at the far end, so there was plenty of room to turn around a wagon. Beyond that area, a set of corrals marked the end of the yard and reached back behind the wagon shed and around to the barn. From the looks of it, unless a person were on foot or on horseback, there was one way in and one way out of this place.

No smoke was rising from the stovepipe of the bunkhouse, so Ed was not surprised that the door did not open as he rode into the narrow end of the yard. He dismounted and knocked on the door, and still no answer came.

Leading the buckskin by the reins, Ed walked to the hitch rack in front of the big house. Looking up, he imagined the gables and dormers as so many brows on a beast, then as so many windows for a spy to look out of. He tied the horse, went up the heavy plank steps, thumped his boots on the porch, and was about to lift the heavy brass knocker when the door opened.

A human form stood inside, and from the appearance, Ed assumed it was not Mort Ramsey. The man stood back from the doorway, and the roof of the porch cut off direct sunlight, but Ed could make out the features well enough. They belonged to a brute of a man, with a large head of the type that scientists liked to measure and study. His hair was close-cropped, like a burr, and his heavy face carried about a week's worth of stubble. He was wearing a heavy, linsey-woolsey pullover shirt with all three buttons missing on the chest. Hanging down from the sleeves of the shirt were a pair of thick hands that looked like mitts with sausages attached. He wore no gunbelt, or belt at all, just a pair of grimy denim trousers that reached down to a pair of clodhopper boots.

Ed took a breath to steel himself. "I'd like to speak to Mr. Ramsey if I could."

The brute turned and motioned with his right hand, showing a set of wide fingernails with black, broken edges.

Ed followed through a dusky front room with scanty furnishings to the doorway of a brighter room where light came in through a side window on the right. It was an office area, with shelves on the left wall, a wide glass-paned gun case in back with a set of deer antlers above, and a hat-and-coat rack in the corner between the gun case and window. In the center of the room sat an oak desk, at least four feet wide and three feet across. At the desk, a man sat with his chin on his left palm, the elbow to one side of some papers he seemed to be studying.

The brute rapped his fingernails on the door panel, and the man looked up. The brute muttered something, and the man leaned his head to one side in order to see past the doorway.

"Good enough, George," he said. "Thanks."

The brute turned and walked away, not going straight past Ed but rather at an angle. As Ed saw his profile, he remembered why the man seemed familiar. He resembled the creature on a playbill for *The Hunchback of Notre-Dame*.

"Come on in," said the man in the office, who had lowered his face to look at the papers again. He had brown hair, thinning on top and greying on the sides.

Ed took off his hat and stepped to the doorway. "Are you Mort Ramsey?"

The man raised his head, fixed his blue eyes with an expression of authority, and said, "Yes, I am. I've been expectin' you. Herm told me about you."

Ed frowned and studied the man, wondering if he himself had missed some link in the sequence. "I'm not sure," he said.

Ramsey maintained his air of command, tensing the muscles on his cheekbone. "You're probably a hand, and Herm speaks well of you, but I don't need a foreman. Bridge does a good job for me. Herm knows that, and I understand he's just passing your question on to me. But that's it. If you want to hire on as a regular hand, that's fine, but if you want to keep looking for something better, there's no hard feelings."

Ed was still trying to make sense of the man and whatever lay behind the blazing blue eyes, the accretion of flesh, and the small broken blood vessels on the florid face. In something of a daze, he found his words. "I'm sorry, but I don't think you've heard of me before. My name's Edward Dawes, and I'm just lookin' for a regular cowpunchin' job."

Ramsey looked him over with half a scowl, then relaxed his face. "Oh. I was expecting—well, it doesn't matter. I just wasn't expecting some other stranger. But that's all right. Tell me again. You're just lookin' to be put on for the season?"

"That's right, sir."

"Where did you work before?"

"Tompkins Ranch, sir, south and east of here."

"I know where it is. Why aren't you going back there to work?"

"I wanted to see some new country."

"Everybody does." His eyes slid over Ed a second time. "You ride out here?"

"Yes, sir."

"So you've got your gear with you?"

"That I do."

Ramsey gave his hard stare. "You know how to take orders?"

"Yes, sir."

"Men come and go at this work. You know what that means?"

Ed shrugged. "Could mean a few things."

"It means no one's indispensable. First time you don't follow orders, you're off the ranch. It's that simple."

"Fine with me. When I ride for another man, I do things his way. It's easier."

"Should be." Ramsey smiled now. "I'll give you a try. What did you say your name is?"

"Ed. Edward Dawes."

"I thought so. Well, I'll tell you what. The other boys are out right now, but you can find an empty bunk in the bunkhouse. You saw it comin' in? First building."

"Yes, sir."

"Go ahead and put your gear in there. If the other boys want you to move to a different cot, go ahead. Bridge knows what's best. Do what he says unless I tell you different."

"All right."

"After you leave off your bedroll, you can put your saddle in the barn and your horse in the corral. You'll see where." He gave Ed the straight look again. "Any questions?"

"I don't think so, Mr. Ramsey."

"Just call me Mort." He stood up and reached his hand across the desk.

As Ed shook his hand, he noticed how the man filled out his shirt and hung over his belt. He might have been a good-looking, husky fellow in his youth, but now he was puffed up like a toad. He gave a smile of assurance and settled back into his chair.

Ed turned and walked out of the office into the dusky front room, which he now saw had a vaulted, open-beam ceiling. George was nowhere in sight, though for all Ed knew, the brute could be lurking in a shadowy corner. Ed crossed the room, opened the door, and put on his hat as he stepped out onto the covered porch. In the light of day, everything looked normal.

He went first to the bunkhouse, where he left his rifle and scabbard, his warbag, and his bedroll on an empty bunk. He did not spend any time inside, as Ramsey had told him he might be re-situated later anyway.

Leading the buckskin to the other end of the yard, he saw that the barn door was now open, as was the door to the other shed. He approached the buildings from several yards out, to see if he might get a look into both before he put away his horse. When the interior of the shed came into view, he saw George the brute standing on the third rung of a ladder and wrapping a chain around a crossbeam. Ed kept leading the horse, and the open doorway of the shed moved out of his view. He stopped at a water trough outside the barn, where he let the animal drink.

Inside the barn, he tied the horse to a stanchion, pulled off the saddle, and set it on a saddle rack that hadn't had any dust worn off it in a while. He laid the sweaty blanket across the saddle, damp side up, to dry out, and he hung the bridle on the saddle horn. Then he led the buckskin out the back door and turned him into the corral.

In no hurry, Ed walked to the north end of the corral and leaned on the top rail, where he could see the back of the ranch house and the bunkhouse. There was not much to be seen. Each building had one back door and an outhouse about twenty feet away. Weeds grew up behind each house, and between the two privies lay a rubbish heap of cans and bottles with an occasional twist of wire, broken water pitcher, or curled boot tossed into the mix.

Ed wandered through the barn and out through the front door, where he stopped short. Mort Ramsey was standing outside the wagon shed and looking in. He was wearing a brown hat, a brown wool vest hanging loose over his full shirt, and a gunbelt. The latter was of dyed brown leather, inlaid with silver conchos on the holster and belt, and holding an ivory-handled six-gun.

Ed took a wide turn to see if he could catch a glimpse inside the shed. As he did, he saw that George had an animal, the size of a yearling steer or heifer, hanging by the hind legs. The carcass had been skinned, and a huge mess of guts was spilling out of the opened abdomen. Ed was amazed at how fast the brute must have worked, unless he had skinned the animal on the ground and then decided to hang it up. Saying nothing to the boss, who took no notice of him, Ed walked back to the bunkhouse.

* * * * *

It came as no surprise to Ed that the man referred to as Herm turned out to be Cooley, Bridge's riding partner. The two of them came into the bunkhouse in the early evening and did not seem to care much about the presence of a new hand. Without saying much, Bridge got up a fire in the stove and heated some leftover beans with a few bloated scraps of pork rind swimming on top. The men sat down to eat, and the two regular hands plied the newcomer with the usual questions of where he came from and where he had worked before. They did not give any indication of having seen him before, and they took little interest in the information he gave about himself.

After supper, Bridge rolled himself a tight cigarette and lit it, while Cooley cut himself a chew of tobacco and then with the same knife took to paring his fingernails. Neither of them had spoken much since they came in, and now Bridge, with the cigarette clamped in his thin lips, told Ed to wash the dishes.

A stack of dirty cups, plates, and silverware from a couple of earlier meals waited for him in the kitchen area, so he had plenty to wash along with the plates, spoons, and pot from the evening meal. Bridge had left a basin of water on the stove, but the fire had died down and the water was barely tepid. Ed set the basin on the table, scattered in some soap flakes, and went to work. Bridge and Cooley sat at the other end of the table, talking about places Ed had not heard of, places where they were going to have to get the calves and cows out for branding.

When he was done with the dishes, Ed asked if he had his gear in a good place. Of the dozen empty bunks, he had picked one at random in the middle.

"Sure," said Bridge, with a flicker of the close-set eyes. "This place'll fill up in a coupla days anyway."

Ed went to his bunk and in a few minutes was settled in. As he stretched out to rest, he glanced at the other end of the room, which was lit by a kerosene lantern. Cooley had taken up a newspaper and was looking at it, while Bridge sat straight up in his chair and held his cigarette between thumb and forefinger on the table in front of him. Smoke rose in a thin ribbon, and Bridge seemed to be reading it.

* * * * *

"Hold that son of a bitch down." Bridge's voice, never loud, came thin and tense across a few feet of space.

Using the rope, Ed pulled the calf's head up off the ground as he sat on the animal's front quarter. Cooley centered his considerable weight on the calf's hind end, and Bridge bent over with the running iron. With a steady hand he burned the brand into the calf's flank as neat as if it had come from the regular branding iron. The smell of burned hair rose in the air, and the calf kicked and bawled.

"Let's cut 'im." Bridge had his pocket knife out, cutting edge up. "Herm, pull those legs apart. And you, haul up on the rope."

Bridge leaned into the task, and a minute later he stood up, flicking the testicles away with his bloody left hand. "That's got it. Now let 'im up."

The three men stood back, and the calf flailed and thrashed until it came to its feet.

Bridge looked at Ed, and still in his low voice, he said, "What the hell you doin'? Take that rope off."

Ed slipped the loop from around the calf's neck, up and over the ears, and past the nose. The calf was a husky one, born at some time between seasons and making it on its own, and it had given some fight. For the moment, though, it seemed dazed, as well it might.

"Let's get goin'," said Bridge, kicking in the little sagebrush fire. "We'll see if we can find that one over by Flat-top."

Ed mounted up and fell in behind the two other men. They seemed to be old hands at mavericking, and Ed guessed they had been waiting for a third man to come along so they could get a few of the larger calves. Ramsey must have told Bridge that the new kid was ready to take orders, because Bridge made no secret of what they were up to, and it figured that he was losing no time to get this work done before the rest of the crew arrived. As for Ed, he was glad for the opportunity to play in.

That evening, Bridge fried beefsteak. Ed recalled the animal he had seen hanging the day before, and he assumed it did not have the King Diamond brand—the two slanted legs of the "K" forming the two left sides of the diamond—that Bridge had so artfully inscribed on the range animals. It didn't matter much, as it was customary to eat beef from other brands, as long as an outfit went about it with discretion, and if a dozen men were about to show up, yesterday's fresh carcass would be down to bones in a few days.

* * * * *

Six of the new men came into the yard the next evening. Ed was sitting in front of the bunkhouse on the wide, flat rock that did for a doorstep, and he saw the men piled in the back of a ranch wagon with their duffel bags and bedrolls. Ed stood up and watched as George pulled the wagon to a stop and Ramsey climbed down from the seat next to him. The boss was dressed as before, with hat and gunbelt, but he had his vest buttoned tight, and a silver watch chain glinted. As he brushed off the road dust, a diamond ring flashed on his left hand.

The new hired men climbed over the sideboards and off the tailgate, some of them stiff and some of them shaky from the long ride. They looked around with wide eyes and, every one of them wordless, trudged into the bunkhouse carrying bags and bedrolls.

Ed had the momentary feeling of being a little superior, having a couple of days' seniority, until Ramsey spoke.

"Here, you. There's a sack of beans and another of rice. Haul them into the kitchen."

The bags weighed a hundred pounds each, and the burlap was rough to the ear as Ed hoisted each one on his shoulder, but he had the work done before some of the men had settled on which cot to take.

Ramsey came into the bunkhouse and approached a man who was loitering at the kitchen end of the long room. "Pat," he said, "you've got to feed these men. There's meat and spuds for tonight. You can cook beans and what-all when you have more time. I'll bring a second load of grub when I go for the rest of the men."

The cook was a slouching man, slender, in a close-fitting pullover sweater and baggy trousers. He nodded and went to work as Ramsey, with his thumb resting on the hammer of his pistol, surveyed his new crew and walked out.

* * * * *

The cook was up and ratting around long before daylight. Ed heard the clunk of firewood in the stove, the scratch of a match, the gurgle of water being poured. After a minute's silence, he felt a hand on his shoulder and heard the cook's voice.

"Hey. Don't you have any bacon grease?"

Ed frowned and opened his eyes. "Bacon grease?"

"Yeah. I need some grease. Where is it?"

"I don't know. Ask Bridge."

"I'm askin' you."

"I just got here a couple of days ago. He did all the cookin'."

"My God, you're as dumb as the rest of 'em."

At breakfast, Pat showed more of his good nature. He must have found the bacon grease, for he set out two heaping platters of shiny fried potatoes and had two skillets crackling with more. "There's coffee, too," he said. "Boil up your insides. Some of you look like you need it. Go without whiskey for a while, maybe you'll be fit to do some work. Now eat up."

The men were going to work with horses out of the corral, and Ed realized that not one of the new men had brought a saddle. This must be quite a crew, he thought. Maybe the cook was right about some of it.

Ed finished his coffee and was rising from his chair when the cook's sharp voice rang out.

"You," he said, pointing at Ed, "and you," pointing at a shaky-looking fellow with dull eyes. "I need the both of you to sort beans. Clear off this end of the table, and go at it. I don't want no clods or rocks."

The other man raised his head and showed a sick look on his face. "Do we have to sort the whole sack?"

"Not yet. I'll tell you how much."

* * * * *

The men had worked two days with the horses, and the second half of the crew came in on the wagon, again without a saddle among them. The next morning after breakfast, Bridge rolled a tight cigarette and crooked his finger at Ed, who had picked his hat off the wall and was about to go out into the morning air.

"You go with Herm today," said the foreman in his steady voice. "I've got my hands full with this new bunch."

Outside in the new daylight, Ed saddled a grey horse from his string and then followed Cooley out of the ranch yard. They rode north about a mile, veered west, followed the base of a low rim for another mile and a half, and stopped at the head of a gully.

"There's one down there that'll do," said Cooley, pointing at a small cluster of cattle.

Ed saw right away that there were two cows, two calves, and one in between that was a yearling or a little better.

"Let's go." Cooley spurred his horse and rode down into the draw.

Ed followed, and within a minute he saw that Cooley wanted to cut out the mid-sized animal, which was a heifer. He could also see that the animals were range-wild, as they bolted in three different directions.

Cooley pounded his horse's flanks and came up on the left side of the heifer, pushing it up the right side of the draw. Ed went after it to haze it on the right, until the animal cut straight across in front of him.

"Rope the bitch!" Cooley hollered.

Ed took down his rope and went after the heifer. As he came up on the left side, he saw a brand as clear as day. It looked like a wigwam with a circle inside it and a dot inside that. Ed did not yet know the brands up in this country, but he knew it sure wasn't the King Diamond. But he also knew he had to make a good showing, so he swung his loop, made his toss, and dallied off.

The heifer jerked around and fought, so Ed held the grey horse in place until the heifer stopped and planted its feet. Rider and animal were still in a standoff when Cooley came riding up.

"Go ahead and take 'er back to the ranch," he said. "George knows what to do with it." He spit out a stream of tobacco juice. "I need to git back and help with that new bunch of men." He kicked his horse and took off on a lope.

Ed was left out in the middle of the big country with someone else's heifer on his rope. He thought it would have been a good way for Cooley to set him up, but he was pretty sure he was not that important to anyone on the King Diamond Ranch—not yet, anyway. Meanwhile, he needed to get this heifer back to the yard before some wandering fool like himself came along.

* * * * *

Within a few days, Bridge and Cooley had pulled together a roundup outfit. Pat ran the chuck wagon just as he ran the kitchen, and the dull-eyed fellow who had helped sort beans became the night wrangler and cook's helper. The man or boy who had that job got the least sleep of anyone, so Tim, as he was called, went in a haze from one day to the next. The others seemed to clear up and get around all right, with the exception of one man who couldn't keep food down. After a few days he rolled his blankets, and a new man took his place.

The new hand went by the name of Hardy, and he was a talkative sort who asked questions and made comments like a village gossip. One day he and Ed rode out together, and as soon as they were out of earshot of the camp, he started his line of chatter. From what he understood, Ramsey got all these men through someone he knew in Cheyenne, who picked 'em up off the street. Ramsey paid 'em cheap, worked 'em hard, and rarely had one back for two years in a row.

"Why do you think that is?" he asked, turning to Ed and looking him straight in the face.

"I don't know. This is only the second place I've worked on."

"What did you do before that?"

"I was a farm boy."

"Do you think you'll be back next year?"

"I have no idea. I'm just gettin' started on this one."

Hardy pursed his lips and then tossed out another question. "What do you know about this fella, Mort Ramsey?"

"Just his name and where he lives."

"Isn't that it? When it comes right down to it, what do you really know about anyone? What you see, and some of what he tells you, but you just don't know which part. Isn't that right?"

"Seems like it."

In a few days, Hardy rolled his blankets and was gone as well. Ed mentioned to Pat that they were going to miss all the friendly talk.

"He's off eatin' at another chuck wagon by now. His type keeps busy."

"Is that right?"

"Yeah. No one else got fired here, so I'd guess he didn't find out anything."

"Is that what he was up to?"

"Pinkerton man, or somethin' just like it. They come in to find out if anyone's doin' anything against the company. Smell 'em a mile away."

Chapter Eight

The interior of the Rimfire Saloon felt like a dusky sanctuary, walled off from the world at large, after the long ride into town. With spring roundup finished, the crew of the King Diamond Ranch had three days off, so Ed had fallen in with six of the other hands to follow Bridge and Cooley on the hot, dusty trail. With his horse in the stable, Ed felt relaxed, cut loose from responsibilities, as he sat with the rest of the boys at the two tables pulled together.

Bridge was being his usual restrained self, not very festive, while Cooley had assumed the role of leader. He had the ebullient air of being at home in his element, and he seemed to have groomed himself for the event. Before leaving the bunkhouse, he had shaved his jowly face and had put on a clean shirt with buttons all the way down the front. Ed noticed that his fingernails were also trimmed and clean. With his large hat at a jaunty angle, he reigned over this little part of the bar-room, wagging his head as he called for drinks and laughed at his own witticisms.

"No, sir, I never have been drunk. Not that I can remember. Har, har, har." Or, "When they ask me if I make good money, I say, sure, it's good, just not enough of it." Humor about drink and money had the inevitable companion. "I said, sure I'll go to the room with you, honey, but let's get one thing straight between us."

Time flowed on. Once when the door opened, Ed saw that night had fallen outside. A few more men had drifted in. Some were standing at the bar, while others had taken a couple of separate tables. Sounds rose and fell in the sea of voices. Ed had finished his first glass of whiskey and was trying to stretch out the second, but he knew it was good form to buy a round, so he did. Now he had two drinks in front of him. The place was hazy with tobacco smoke and lamp light. Two of the King Diamond punchers drifted off, so Cooley got everyone around one table.

From time to time, someone would lean into the company of the King Diamond table and make a sociable comment. Smiles would go around the table, including a thin one from Bridge, and Cooley would answer. One man seemed to take it too far, as Cooley rose to his feet with a backward scrape of his chair and grabbed the man's shirt front. Ed did not hear the original comment, but Cooley's gravelly voice carried loud and clear above the din.

"Men get killed for sayin' things like that."

The other man tried to shrink back as he turned his head aside. He was a soft-looking man of about thirty with clean clothes and hat and a yellow neckerchief, and Ed thought he recognized him as a windmill salesman.

"I'm sorry," said the man, still cowering and no doubt expecting to be hit or slapped.

"That's not enough."

"I said I'm sorry."

"Sorry's not enough."

The man eyes were wavering and searching. "What else do you want?"

"Take it back."

The man's eyes held still. "I'm sorry. I take it back. I didn't mean it. It was just in fun."

"That kind of talk isn't funny."

"I know that now. I'm sorry. I didn't mean it."

Cooley relaxed his grip on the man's ironed shirt. "Go away. Count yourself lucky."

The man disappeared, and Cooley sat down, shaking his head.

"What did he say?" Ed asked the puncher on his right, whose name was Al.

"Something about horse thieves. He thought he was just joshin'."

Ed drew back into himself. He was going to have to be careful. Cooley could blow up at anything, but there was Bridge to look out for as well. He didn't call much attention to himself, sitting there with his lips stretched over his teeth and the corners of his mouth showing. Ed closed his eyes and opened them. He told himself again he was going to have to be careful, keep his mouth shut, and fit in.

After a while, another man emerged from the haze. He stood by Cooley's chair, slapping him on the shoulder and yuk-yukking. The man seemed out of place to Ed, and yet he didn't. His eyes traveled around the table and stopped.

"Well, who have we got here?" he sang out. "Hello, Ed."

"Hello, Jeff."

"Doin' any good?"

Ed half-closed his eyes as he nodded. "All right."

Jeff, with his right hand still on Cooley's shoulder, waved toward Ed with his left. "This young fella worked under me last year," he said. "Bound to make a good hand. I didn't know he was workin' for you-all."

"He's good," said Cooley. "We got a bunch."

"Need 'em all, I bet. Have a good calf crop?"

"Damn good. And yourself?"

"Oh, yeah. I just wish I had a couple more good men, but we do with what we've got."

"Have to." Cooley looked around the table. "Can I buy you a drink?"

"Just one." Jeff tipped his hat back. "Better yet, let me buy a round." He made a circular motion with his finger.

Ed put his hand over his two drinks. "No more for me, thanks. I've got plenty."

"Hah-hah," said Jeff. "I forgot, Ed doesn't like to have fun. But that's all right. That's why you don't have any trouble with him. Isn't that right, Ed?"

"I guess so."

Jeff stood by the table until the drinks came and he paid for them. "I'll see you a little later on," he said, patting Cooley on the shoulder again. "I've got to look after my own bunch."

"Thanks for the drinks," said Cooley.

"My pleasure." Jeff smiled around the table as the others thanked him. He nodded at Bridge, who barely returned the gesture, and then he left.

Cooley looked in Ed's direction and called across the table. "I didn't know you knew Jeff. Why does he say you don't like to have fun?"

"He couldn't get me to play dominoes."

"Is that all? Did he usually win?"

"Probably his share of the time. I don't remember. I didn't pay much attention."

"We're havin' fun now, though, aren't we?"

"Oh, yeah. You damn right." Ed held up his glass in salute, then took a drink.

Time buzzed on. Ed lapsed into himself again, and he realized he hadn't had anything to eat since breakfast. That was why the whiskey was going to his head. He must have had four or five by now. He sure couldn't go to Mrs. Porter's like this, but he wished he could order something to eat somewhere. He asked Al, the puncher next to him, what he thought, and Al said they were all going to the parlor.

"What parlor?"

"The one with girls. Herm says he'll show us the place."

"Can we get somethin' to eat there?"

"I don't know. I'll ask." Al raised his voice and said, "Herm, he wants to know if he can get somethin' to eat where we're goin'."

"Sure. He can order anything there. Come on, finish your drinks, fellas, and we'll go spread some legs." Cooley drank down the last of his own glass and stood up. "Come on, Ed. We'll show you what some fun is."

Ed tossed off the rest of his drink and stood up. He felt woozy when he was on his feet, but he steadied himself and looked around at the group. Bridge had gone off somewhere, and the other two punchers hadn't come back. That made six—Cooley, the four remaining King Diamond punchers, and Ed. With Cooley in the lead, they all clomped out of the saloon and into the night. Ed reminded himself what town he was in, then kept track of the way as Cooley took them past the livery stable to the corner, a block north, and then a block and a half west. After a little commotion at the front door of a building, they all went in.

Ed found himself in a good-sized front room with three divans, a small upright piano, and a bar against the back wall. Women were mingling with the new patrons. Ed counted. There was a tall man behind the bar serving drinks, a madam sitting on a high stool at the end of the bar, and three women talking in loud voices to the men.

Cooley appeared in front of him. "Five dollars."

"What?"

"Give me five dollars."

"What for?"

"It's five dollars each. All you can drink and all you can hump for three hours."

Ed felt his head drifting as he leaned forward and straightened up.

"We're all going into the other room. These three girls and us. They're gonna do it all. If you've got it in you, you can do all three. That and the liquor, all for the same money."

Ed took a deep breath and held his head up. "I wanted to get somethin' to eat."

"Order it from in there. Now c'mon, give me the five dollars."

After a little fumbling, Ed found the right coin and gave it to him. Someone handed him a drink.

The next room had only one lamp, turned down low, and people were moving around. Al leaned against the wall, standing on one foot and pulling the boot off the other. The door opened, and light spilled in from the other room. Ed could see two beds with brass railings, with bodies on both, in the room where he found himself. The tall man came in with a thin mattress and flopped it on the floor. He closed the door on the way out, and then Cooley came in and left it open.

One of the women stood in front of Ed. He could see her light-colored hair and eyes, her narrow nose, and her mouth that looked like a dark pit when she talked.

"Are you going to go first, sweetie?" She rubbed the front of his pants.

"I wanted to get something to eat. I'm hungry."

"In here?"

"They told me I could order something."

"Not here, honey. We order everything from the café, and it closed a couple of hours ago."

"Then I need to sit down."

"There's a chair over there. Be careful you don't fall."

He found the chair, a stuffed armchair, and he settled into it. Someone put a drink in his hand, but he didn't know if it was his or someone else's for him to hold. He thought maybe he drank the other one.

He heard rustling, shifting of bodies, heavy breathing, a man's cough, and low voices.

"Don't do that," said a woman with a nasal voice.

A slapping sound of a man's hand on flesh. A man's voice. "Is that you, Bill?"

"I wondered who that was."

"Didn't mean to interrupt you. Keep at it."

Then the woman's voice again, from another place. "I said don't do that."

With great effort, Ed set the drink on the floor. He leaned back and closed his eyes. A few minutes later, someone was shaking his shoulder.

"Go take your turn, Ed."

He wasn't sure whose voice it was, but he answered, "Not yet."

"Where's my drink?"

"I set it on the floor."

The woman with the nasal voice spoke again. "Oh, it's you."

Cooley's gravelly voice answered. "Who'd you think it was, Grover Cleveland?"

"Not when I felt the size of you." She gave a lewd laugh.

The man at his elbow spoke again. Ed couldn't remember who it was, but he thought it was Al. The man said, "Come on, Ed. Go take your turn. I'll sit in the chair."

Ed shook his head. "Not right now."

The man moved away.

The door opened, light fell on a tangle of bare legs, and the door closed. Ed relaxed his eyes.

Someone was shaking him by the shoulder, and he woke up. He heard Cooley's voice. "Here, have a drink."

From deep down, Ed remembered he was supposed to be having fun, fitting in with the gang. "Thanks," he said.

"And when you're done with the girls, pour some of this down the eye of your peter. It'll kill all the germs."

"I'll do that."

* * * * *

Ed woke up in the grey light. A horse had just snuffled. Opening his eyes, he saw the reddish hind legs of a sorrel. He gave a sideways glance toward his cheekbone and saw that he was sleeping in straw. He had made it back to the livery stable.

He was glad to know it. He realized he had just come up out of a dream. Cooley was there, in a stovepipe hat and a long black coat, waving a black walking stick to lead on a throng of demon-like men, also dressed in black. They were all down in a maze of dungeons, clambering over rocks and going around pillars. Ed had been running from them, hiding in nooks and then running again, never making enough progress. In his dream, he knew the way to the surface world but couldn't make it there. He kept stopping like a fool.

He heaved out a long, slow breath. It was good to know that it had been just a dream, although he still felt paralyzed. He didn't know how much whiskey he had drunk, but it had been way too much, and he wasn't used to it. Now it flowed in his veins like a toxin. He felt rotten, and he wished he could lie flat on the hard dirt floor of the stable and let the earth draw the poison out of him.

* * * * *

Ed woke again. In spite of how miserable he felt, he knew he couldn't stay huddled in the straw but was going to have to go out into the world. He couldn't go to the boarding house until he got straightened out, but he needed to eat. He thought of the café, which was about a block away, and he hoped he could get a meal there without running into any of the crew from last night.

Much to his relief, he didn't know anyone in the café. He sat at a small corner table, where he ate a full meal of steak and fried potatoes, washed down with four cups of coffee. As he stepped out onto the street, he felt much better than he did when he went in, but he still had a dull, detached feeling that he was stumbling along half-outside himself.

He was starting to sweat, and he took it as a good sign that his boiler was going to work. Although he felt restless and could have walked five miles even in his boots, he thought he needed to hole up for a while. Of the places he could think of, Tyrel Flood's seemed like a good choice.

After knocking on the door and going in as commanded, he found the old man seated at the kitchen table. Tyrel had a knife stuck upright in the table top, and the last remnants of a hambone, including a few scraps of rind, lay on a crockery platter.

"How goes it with the young wanderer?" The brown eyes were quick if not bright.

"All right, I suppose. Could be better."

"Bad luck?"

Ed shook his head. "No, just bad judgment."

"Ha-ha!" The old man's narrow teeth showed. "It's happened before." His voice changed as he said, "Hey, you get out of there." He rapped his knuckles on the skull of the brown-and-yellow cat, which had climbed up on the other chair and was pushing its nose at the ham scraps. "That's goin' into a pot of beans. Go catch a mouse."

The cat settled back on the chair, squinting its eyes in what looked like a frown. The old man tipped the back of the chair so that the cat slid off.

"Here, sit down, and tell me about your great misfortune."

Ed sank into the chair and let out a weary breath. "Got drunk last night."

"It's happened before. To better men than either of us, if you don't mind my sayin' so."

"Not at all, especially the way I feel." Ed shook his head. "I don't usually drink much. Not because I'm all that pure. I just don't care much for it."

"Some people are like that. Strange, but you see it." Tyrel winced as he shifted in his seat. "Did you get payday drunk?"

"I suppose so. I came into town with Herm Cooley and the bunch. I imagine you knew I went to work for them."

"I'd heard it."

"Well, we rode into town in late afternoon, early evenin', and we all went to the Rimfire. We must have been there till midnight, and then we went to a parlor house. I was so gone I couldn't even stand up."

"That's too bad. But sometimes a fella just loses control. If it's any comfort, you probably weren't the only one."

"Oh, no. Just the stupidest." Ed did not mention that at least at the time, he had hoped that going along with the bunch would help him keep his cover at the King Diamond Ranch. "But you're right. The others were like swine, too."

"Was Bridge there?"

"He was with us when we were in the saloon, but he disappeared somewhere along the way."

"That's like him. He'll slip off and not be in the middle of the big mess. He'll be clear-eyed in the mornin', while all the rest of those rannies are sick as dogs."

"He seems like a cautious one."

"Stays out of the way, a good part of the time. Before he took to ridin' with Cooley, they say he never traveled back the same way he came."

"You mean when he came into town?"

"Anywhere he went. I don't think he's changed any. If he goes somewhere by himself now, he probably still has the same moves."

"Cagey."

"That's right. You won't find him gettin' into a hole where there's only one way out." Tyrel laughed. "Cooley, on the other hand, you might find him in any of a variety of holes."

Ed's thoughts drifted. "I was wonderin'. Does Grover Cleveland wear a stovepipe hat?"

"Oh, I'm sure he does. Probably been known to wear a derby as well. But when they're formal and presidential, they wear the stovepipes. Why?"

"Just a thought."

"One among many." Tyrel took hold of his stick and pushed himself up from his chair. "Let me get us some coffee."

Ed noticed the old man's sagging build. Tyrel wasn't fat, but his belt curved under his gut, and his clothes hung on him like old hand-me-downs.

"I can get it," Ed offered.

"Nah, I will. I need to get up and around once in a while." The old man set two cups on the table and poured them full. "Do you want anything to eat?"

"No, thanks. I ate a little while ago. What I really need is to get this poison out of my system."

Tyrel let out a heavy sigh as he sank into his chair. "Yesterday's wine," he said. Pointing at the hambone, he added, "Today's meat. All gone but the residue and scraps. Who knows what tomorrow's bread will be like?" His old brown eyes played over Ed. "Here I am, talkin' in runes, and all you wish is your head would clear up. Don't worry. You're young. You'll feel a hell of a lot better tomorrow."

* * * * *

After two cups of coffee and a fair sampling of Tyrel's philosophy, Ed felt the need to get off on his own and see if he could clear his head any better. He didn't have to leave for the ranch until the following morning, so he had time to visit Ravenna later on. Meanwhile, he still wanted to avoid anyone from the King Diamond.

He decided to take his horse from the stable and go for a ride. The air and the sun and the exertion might wear off some of the ragged edges. The ride would take him out of town, and as long as he didn't go north, he should be all right.

The sun had climbed halfway up in the sky when he rode east out of Litch. He figured he would ride until the sun was straight up, and then he would turn around and come back. If he kept to the road, he wouldn't attract any special attention.

The ride out was uneventful enough. Before turning back, he dismounted to check his cinch and stretch his legs. After mounting up again and setting out on the return, he saw two riders and four horses coming his way. A couple of minutes later, he saw that the horsemen were Jory Stoner and Homer Dugdale, and each had an unsaddled horse on the end of his rope.

Ed reined his horse and drew him off to the side of the trail as Jory and Homer came up to him.

"Howdy, pal," Jory sang out. "Where you comin' from?"

"Just out for a ride and on my way back." Ed shook his head. "Had too much to drink last night."

"Had some fun, huh?" Jory's teeth flashed as he smiled.

"Too much. Or the wrong kind. Must be the company I've fallen into. Not the good influence I had with you two."

Homer smiled at the compliment. "We heard you went to work for the King Diamond. I hope it's been all right for you."

"Oh, it'll do. I don't think I'll stay there forever."

"Whatever suits." Homer gave a little shrug.

Ed felt a brief pang of guilt, then thought of an easier topic. "Say, I'll tell you who I ran into. That fella Jeff that worked with us last year."

Homer nodded. "He's workin' for an outfit over your way."

"Talks like he's a foreman. As far as that goes, he let on that I worked for him last year."

"Maybe he thinks you did." A shine came to Homer's faraway blue eyes. "He wanted to be foreman for Cal, and when he didn't get it, he went off in a huff. You remember that."

"I didn't know why he left so quick. Reuben said his money was burnin' a hole in his pocket."

"Oh, some of it was impatience, and some of it was from Cal turnin' him down."

"Huh. So do you know if he's a foreman now?"

"I don't believe he is, but he's still mindin' the main chance."

"Well, he was friendlier to me than I would have expected, and I don't have a job for him."

"Sometimes they're that way just for the practice. But I've probably said more than I need to."

Jory spoke. "How about—?" With raised eyebrows and a close-mouthed smile, he waved his head and the broad brim of his hat backwards.

"Oh, it's goin' along."

"Haven't rode off with her yet? That's what you ought to do. Get out of the bad company, too, all at once. Then they won't be keepin' you out till all hours and makin' your head hurt."

"Well, it's not their fault. And besides, like I said, I don't expect to be a permanent fixture there anyway. I'm puttin' in my time until I move on to the next thing."

"If you've got half a plan, that's better than most."

"I hope I do." Ed looked from one rider to another. "Well, it's been good seein' you boys. Does me good. But I probably need to be gettin' back."

Jory smiled and wagged his hat again.

"So long," said Homer. "It's good to see you, too. If you get out our way, drop in. Meanwhile, take care of yourself, and look out for them other fellas."

"I will."

* * * * *

By the time he had his horse put away and walked to the boarding house, Ed was too late to talk to Ravenna. She was already at work on the evening meal. Now at loose ends, he went back to the stable and dozed for an hour. After that, he washed up, ate supper at the café, and returned to the boarding house to wait for Ravenna.

It was well after dark when she finished her work, and the house was still hot inside, so she suggested that they sit on the back porch. They sat on the back steps for a couple of minutes without saying anything until she spoke.

"You didn't just get into town this afternoon, did you?"

"No. I came in yesterday with a bunch of the other boys."

"That's what I thought I heard, that some men from your ranch had come in."

"We did. I stayed with them and went to the saloon, and then I got stuck there. I drank too much, and I was sick like a dog this morning, so I thought I'd wait until I was more presentable."

"You don't usually do that, do you?"

"No, and I don't enjoy it, either. If I'd gotten to town a little sooner or a little later, I could have come over here, but it was in the late afternoon, and then I got stuck. By the way, who did you hear it from that we'd come in?"

"A man who stays here once in a while. He mentioned it at breakfast."

"Not the fella who sells windmills?"

"No, it was a man who works at one of the ranches. His name is Jeff."

Ed felt a wave of dread. "He didn't mention my name, did he?"

"No. Do you know him?"

"If he's the fella I think he is. A few years older than me, a little heavier build. Acts like he's a foreman. Comes from Arkansas."

"That's him."

"I worked with him last year, and now he's over here. I saw him in the winter, but I don't think he ever stayed here then, did he?"

"No, I think it's been the last month or six weeks."

"Just don't pay him any mind, is the best."

"I try not to, but it seems he's there every time I turn around."

Ed felt an uneasiness spreading through him. "You mean he hangs around?"

"Yes. And his eyes go everywhere. I think he might even peep."

"Have you seen him at it?"

"No, but I've heard noises, right outside."

"That's not good. But you can't very well ask Mrs. Porter not to let him stay here. Not till you have more."

"I know. But I don't like it. He reminds me of Mr. Gregory. You know I mentioned him."

Ed felt his pressure going up inside. "The farmer back in Crete."

"Yes. I wish he would just go away."

"I know what you mean, but it doesn't always work out the way you want."

They sat in silence for a couple of minutes until she spoke again. "So, have things gone well for you in your work?"

"You mean punchin' cows?"

"Well, that."

"Oh, it's been all right, I suppose. I liked it better at the ranch where I worked last year, but I'm workin' on a plan, so I can put up with a lot of little things."

"That's good." After a few seconds, she added, "And the plan? Have you found out anything?"

"Not to speak of. The first fella I mentioned plays everything real close to his chest, and I get the feeling I could wait a thousand years before someone dropped a comment I was hopin' for. But at least I'm gettin' to know him a little better, just by seein' his habits."

"And the other one?"

"Oh, the big boss. Mort Ramsey. No, I haven't gotten to know much about him at all. I need to learn more, and I'm not sure how to get close enough to do it."

"Well, I hope you find out. If he did something that wasn't right—"

He found her hand with his. Up until this moment they had both been looking forward into the darkness, and now they turned to each other.

"I know," he said, and their lips met in a kiss. For a moment he lost himself, as if he were floating with her in the night sky, and then he came back to the here and now. He held his lips close to her ear and said, "I know. And as soon as I'm done with all of it, we can do more of this."

Their lips met again as they put their arms around one another, two orphans under a dark sky, on the back steps of a boarding house.

Chapter Nine

Ed sat in the dark in back of Mrs. Porter's establishment, wondering when the moon was going to rise. When it did, he was going to have to find shadow, but it would help him see if anyone came lurking tonight. He didn't like the idea that Jeff came around to peep, and even though the man had not kept his room for this night, he still might be in town.

The darkness began to thin before he saw the moon itself, a pale, three-quarters disc beginning to show above the roof of the building across the alley. Unless he sat right in front of the outhouse, this clump of hollyhocks would give as good a shadow as anything on Mrs. Porter's lot. He scooted over a few feet and stayed sitting, Indian fashion, as he watched the boarding house.

He was beginning to tire of his position and was thinking of shifting when a movement at the right side of the building caught his eye. Holding himself motionless, he saw the figure move as if a person had taken a slow step. In less than a minute, Ed saw that it indeed was a person, coming from the north side of the house and making stealthy progress toward the steps to the back porch. Ed pushed himself forward to his knees, and when the intruder was halfway across the length of the building, Ed rose up and spoke.

"Hold it right there," he said.

The person stopped.

As Ed covered the few remaining yards, he could see it was Jeff. "I'm not surprised," he said.

"Neither am I," came the answer. Jeff spoke in his sarcastic drawl. "I come out here to look for prowlers, and see what I get."

"I think you've got it backwards. I was on the lookout, and you're the one sneakin' around."

Jeff's voice took on a more menacing tone. "Be careful what you say, boy. Words can get you in trouble."

"So can actions."

"What do you mean by that?"

"Well, it's clear as day that you're trespassin' at night in a place where—"

A smashing fist on the left side of his face kept Ed from finishing the sentence. As he staggered back a step and tried to keep his balance, a second punch connected on his right side. He was trying to bring his fists up when a third punch knocked him to the ground. He fell on his right hip and shoulder, and as he tried to push himself up, the toe of a boot stabbed pain into the upper part of his left arm. Then he heard a revolver click.

"Just stay where you are, boy, and you won't get hurt any more. But let this be a lesson. You need to be careful about what you say. Here I am, tryin' to look out for a poor widda lady, and some boy prowlin' in the night pulls a gun on me."

"I didn't pull a gun. You did."

"I do what I have to, to protect myself. Take it to her if you want to, and it's your word against mine. I'll tell her how it happened, including how I knocked you flat on your ass." This last word he pronounced "aiss," with a note of emphasis. Then he turned and walked away in the night.

Ed sat up and felt both sides of his face. He didn't feel anything out of order, but he didn't like the turn things had taken. He remembered the adage that the first liar didn't have a chance, and even though he wouldn't be lying, Jeff would do his best to make it out that way. Ed could see that nothing good would come from bringing up this incident with Mrs. Porter, but now that it had happened, Jeff might lay off his peeping.

Then there was Ravenna. Embarrassing as it might be, Ed was going to have to tell her about it so she would know. Furthermore, if Jeff did bring it up later and try to distort it, at least Ed would have gotten in the first version with someone. As he pushed himself to his feet, he told himself he was going to have to do better than this in the future.

* * * * *

Ed left for Thunder Basin early the next morning and did not waste time, arriving at the valley of ancient dead cottonwoods in early afternoon. He watered the buckskin and then crossed the creek bottom to find a pine tree big enough to give shade. He loosened the cinch on the horse and sat on the hillside to rest.

This valley seemed never to change. The hill he sat on would change color from evening to morning, but it would change just as it did a year ago. The tops of the dead cottonwoods looked the same, as did the vast colony of abandoned prairie dog holes. Maybe a tree had fallen, or tumbleweeds had blown in or out of the mouths of some of the burrows, but to Ed the place seemed timeless. He could believe that it looked just like this before his name was Dawes.

The buckskin was stamping, moving his head to one shoulder and the other, swishing his tail. The flies hadn't taken long to find him, and there wasn't much rest for a horse being nettled. Left to themselves, horses would run from one end of a pasture to another, just to escape the flies for a little while. When the bugs weren't quite that thick, two horses would stand head to tail and swish the bugs off one another. But the buckskin didn't have those options at the moment, and Ed figured it was time to move on.

He stood up, coiled the rope, and slipped it off the horse's neck and over the head. He could see the flies, little white ones that gathered around the ears and eyes and on the upper chest. After tying the rope onto the saddle, he brushed at the flies, trying to dislodge them where they had already dug in. Blood smeared in his fingers, but he got rid of a few. Leading the buckskin out into the sunlight and onto a level spot, he tightened the cinch and swung aboard. With a touch of the spurs, he put the valley behind him.

* * * * *

At the bunkhouse, Pat the cook told him that Cooley and a couple of the other hands hadn't come back from town, but Bridge had the rest of them out cutting hay and probably wouldn't get in till dark. Ed put his horse away, thinking that everyone was supposed to have this day off as well. The sun was slipping into the latter part of the afternoon, and the shadows were starting to stretch, so he went to the front door of the bunkhouse and sat on the wide, flat rock that served as the doorstep. The door was open, as the bunkhouse heated up at this time of day, and Ed could hear the cook rummaging around. No matter, Ed thought. He had made good time so as not to get back late, and he was going to rest while he could.

Before long, however, he saw George the brute go up the front steps of the ranch house, and a few minutes later, Mort Ramsey came out. He crossed the area of bare dirt and stood about five feet from where Ed sat.

The boss of the King Diamond Ranch was dressed in the style he used when he went out to order his men around. He wore his hat, his brown vest, a clean white shirt with full buttons, his silver watch chain, and his silver inlaid gunbelt with the ivory-handled six-gun. Squeezed into this outfit, and in places bulging out of it, was the boss himself. He was not fat like a storekeeper or a German farmer but rather like a person who was swollen up all over.

The florid face and puffy hands put Ed in mind of a story that Emerson the blacksmith had told him about a man who ate a peach and got a hornet in his mouth. He was stung a few times before he could get the hornet out, and the poison spread through him. His face and neck and hands swelled up, and his throat closed almost to the point of choking him to death. Emerson said it was a sight to see, like a dog that got bit by a snake, and he liked to tell the story.

Ed looked up at the boss.

"You don't look like you're very busy," said Ramsey.

"I'm bound to go in and help the cook any time now."

"What's he got for you?"

"Ah, there's always somethin'."

Ramsey lifted his chin and looked around. "Where's Bridge?"

"I think he's still out with the crew."

"Well, I need a man to do a job. It'll take a little while, so maybe it'll have to wait till tomorrow." He focused his stare downward on Ed. "You see, I'm going to be bringing a new bride onto the ranch, and I need a few things cleaned up."

"That sounds wonderful, sir. I'm happy for you."

"So am I. But I need to get things ready."

"Of course."

"I've got a bunch of old things to burn. Mostly papers, but some other things as well. A couple of broken chairs, some old crates, that sort of thing." He waved with his left hand, and his diamond ring flashed.

"That might take a while, if you don't mind my saying so, sir. I could get an early start on it in the morning, though, and get it done before any wind comes up."

Ramsey looked around and off in the distance again. "Some of this stuff is in the cellar. George could show you where it is, and you could haul it up tonight. Have everything ready."

Ed did not like the feeling he was getting from the conversation. He looked past Ramsey and saw George, hatless as always, standing in the shadows of the ranch-house porch. Coming back to Ramsey, Ed saw the man gazing away with a spiteful expression on his face, as if the last thing on his mind was his new bride.

"Sounds like a good idea, sir."

"What's that?"

"Burn this trash in the morning, but get it ready now. I could get out of cuttin' up all those spuds, which I hate anyway. I'll go tell Pat." Ed stood up.

"Nah. You go ahead and do the kitchen work. We can do this other job tomorrow. Have you seen Herm?"

"Not at all. I thought he was out with Bridge." Ed hoped Pat didn't hear him.

Ramsey shook his head. "I don't think so." Then, looking at Ed as if he were a perfect fool, he said, "Go in and help the cook."

Ed did as he was told, making short work of the potatoes and leaving them in a gleaming white pile. He laid down his knife, put a pained expression on his face, and said, "I've got to go out back."

He put on his hat and left through the back door toward the outhouse, but instead of going in, he went around it and scrambled up the hillside. As he climbed, he thought about Ramsey, Bridge, and circumstances in general. Something always seemed wrong at the King Diamond Ranch, and it seemed even more so at the present. Thinking he might see something if he watched the ranch yard for a while, he took a seat where a small outcropping of rocks gave a little shade and might absorb his form.

Nothing moved in the yard below. He assumed Ramsey and George were in the big house, but he had no idea of what they might be up to. Going into the cellar with George had struck Ed as ominous, and he wondered how much of the story about the bride and the cleanup was real. Ed figured he might find out in the morning.

Still nothing moved in the yard. Lifting his gaze and scanning the higher land, Ed saw something that gave him a jolt. A man on horseback was coming out of the high brush on the trail in from the main road and was riding south toward headquarters. Ed articulated the form that he had already recognized. It was Cooley.

Ed kept still and hoped Cooley wouldn't see him. He decided that as soon as Cooley rode past the bunkhouse, this spot would be out of view. He could scamper down the hillside, in through the back door, and be rattling plates while Cooley was putting his horse away.

His luck didn't hold out, though. The blocky rider's hatbrim went up, and in the next moment, Cooley was trotting the brown horse up and across the slope toward the outcropping of rocks.

Ed kept his seat. If he stood up, he would have a better pull at his gun, but he hoped that wouldn't be necessary. Meanwhile, there were a few rocks at hand that were smaller than George's head and might be useful if it came to that.

The hoofbeats sounded on the dry ground as the big-hatted rider came closer. The horse was sweating along the neck and around the saddle blanket, and specks of froth showed on the bit. Dust rose as Cooley pulled the horse to a stop.

Ed hoped the man would make fun of him for getting drunk and not taking his turns at the parlor house, but Cooley's meaty face carried a sour expression, and his gravelly voice had a sharp tone.

"What are you doin' up here spyin'?"

Ed widened his eyes. "Not spyin' at all. Came up here to see if I could catch a breeze. Hotter'n hell in the bunkhouse, and I just cut up a heap of spuds. Ask Pat."

"I don't have to ask Pat a damn thing. I'm askin' you."

"Well, I told you all there is to tell."

Cooley swung down from his horse, seemed to miss his balance on his bootheels, and caught it. He was standing downhill from where Ed sat and was at almost the same eye level. He took a heavy breath and said, "You haven't told me what I asked."

"I'm sorry, but I did."

Cooley pulled off his riding gloves and stuffed them in his vest pocket as he spoke, rough as always. "Listen here, you little son of a bitch. I don't like snoops. Nobody does. So out with it, before I beat you to a pulp."

"I don't know what you're getting at."

The big man's lower lip hung down, and a fleck of saliva jumped out as he said, "The hell you don't. I want to know what you're spyin' on."

"Well, to tell you the truth, I'm lookin' out for you."

Cooley frowned. "The hell you are."

"The hell I'm not. That fella you shook up in the Rimfire the other night, he's plenty mad at you. I heard he bought a box of rifle shells and was headed out this way."

"You really are stupid, aren't you, to think I'd believe that."

"Why not? It's the truth. Ask anyone in town."

"Ask Pat. He knows as much about it way out here."

"Don't take my word for it, then."

"I damn sure won't, and you're gonna answer my question if I have to shake you till your teeth rattle." Cooley's own lower teeth showed as he spoke.

"I've told you as much as I can. That fella's got a vengeance."

"Forget that fairy tale. You know what I'm gettin' at."

"Not yet."

"Well, I'll tell you. You're nothin' but a no-good little spy, and I know it."

"If you think I'm like that fellow Hardy, you're wrong."

Cooley had his tongue between his lips, then drew it back. "I don't know what kind you are, but I know you're a snoop."

"That's more than I know."

Cooley's face grew hard, and he seethed. "Look here, kid. You've got one more chance, and then I'm going to smear you on this hillside."

"All right. I'll answer anything."

The big man' words came slow and strained, as if through clenched teeth. "I want to know what you want to dig up about Mort Ramsey."

As Ed heard the words, the world around him began to swim—Cooley and the brown horse downhill in front of him, the hazy sky beyond them in the distance, the ranch headquarters below. He pulled in a breath and said, "How did you know?"

"Never mind how I know. But you want to find out something about Mort Ramsey, and I want to know what, and why. Now you can tell me, or you can let George get it out of you."

Jeff. That's who it had to be. He must have been listening earlier, when Ed and Ravenna were talking. It was the only time Ed had said that name out loud. There would have been plenty of time between the moment of the one-sided fistfight and the time Cooley left town. And Jeff would have loved passing it on.

"How do I know you won't beat me up and then give me to George anyway? I might as well get one beating instead of two."

"To tell you the truth, I don't care. Now quit stallin'."

"All right. It went like this. Hardy told me the boss had it in for one of his top men. That didn't sound fair to me, so I thought if I could find out which one—"

Cooley reached over to grab Ed by the shirt. His grasp missed as Ed moved, and he grabbed again. "Damn you, I've had enough of your—"

"Look out! There's a snake!" Ed's words were sharp as he pulled his feet up under him.

By reflex, Cooley turned in his stooped position. Ed pulled free, and with his right hand, he brought a rock up and around, then down on the back of Cooley's head. It stumbled the man and knocked his hat off. Ed hit him again, and Cooley went to his hands and knees. Ed dropped the rock and with both hands picked up a larger one. As Cooley lifted his right hand and reached back for his pistol, Ed brought the rock down on the base of Cooley's skull and laid him out.

The world was quiet again. The horse had snuffled and snorted, run about thirty yards, and stopped where it now stood with the reins trailing. Down in the ranch yard, nothing stirred.

Everything came to mind at once, and Ed had to take a deep breath as he tried to get his thoughts in order. Cooley had just come from town, and he had not yet talked with either Bridge or Ramsey. That meant he hadn't told anyone what he heard from Jeff, or at least what he had developed as an urgent theory since the night in the parlor house. Meanwhile, Bridge had to have come back yesterday if he took a crew out today, so he wouldn't have heard it in town, much less here. Still, Ed wondered if Ramsey had heard something. Wanting Ed to go into the cellar with George sounded suspicious, but as Ed reasoned it out, Ramsey wouldn't have told him that much if he was really onto him, and he wouldn't have told Ed to go in and help the cook.

Ed was trying to settle down his breathing. He was taking a few minutes to absorb the idea that he had just clobbered the big man to death, but he needed to act fast. He couldn't stay out on this hillside with a dead man and his horse in plain view.

As Ed went for the brown horse, he tried again to pull himself together and get things in their places. Ramsey and the brute were in the big house, and Pat was in the bunkhouse. Cooley would not have come within their view before he turned off and came this way. If Bridge had taken a crew of men to cut hay, they were off to the southwest, and they wouldn't have seen Cooley come in, either. That left two men unaccounted for, the ones who hadn't come back yet from town. Unless they knew that Cooley set out ahead of them, no one knew where he was—except Ed. He needed to keep it that way, and he couldn't waste time or effort.

First, the hat. He mashed it down with his boot soles, then stuffed it under the slicker tied on the back of Cooley's saddle. He took down the rope, looped it around Cooley's chest and snugged it under the armpits, tied it to the saddle horn, and led the horse by the reins. The brown was a good ranch horse and had dragged plenty of steers, so he leaned into the weight and went to work.

After a couple of hundred yards, the land began to slope downhill, and Ed stopped the horse when he could no longer see to the south and west. Relieved to be closed off from view, he took a minute to catch his breath. He was out in the middle of a huge grassland, with no trees for miles, and he couldn't drag this body as he had done with the deer. For one thing, he didn't have a carpet of snow, and for another, he didn't want to leave a trail. He needed to get the body loaded on the horse, and he still had no time to lose.

Cooley was wearing a belt in addition to his gunbelt, so Ed took off the regular belt and, winding it around the horse's ankles and buckling it, he made a set of hobbles. He positioned the horse so that the body lay along its left side not far from its hooves, and he took the rope off to get it out of the way. Then he tried to lift the body. At first the shifting, dead weight seemed impossible, but Ed concentrated his strength and made a little more progress each time. After about five tries, he got the dead man's chest onto the seat of the saddle, and from there he was able to hook the left arm around the saddle horn. With a deep breath, he secured a new grip, then pushed and lifted until he had the load slung across so he could tie it down. He did not like treating the body the way he had to in order to get it tied off so it wouldn't slip, but he told himself it was only a body now, and his work was just a task.

When he was satisfied that the load wasn't going to shift and fall off, he unwrapped the hobbles and set out leading the horse. He went north to some broken country he knew of, and when he found a crevice that was wide and deep enough, he untied the burden and pushed it in. He tossed the belt and hat in on top.

He had made sure that both gloves stayed in the man's vest pocket, and now he gave the saddle a careful looking over. No blood stains were visible, so he set off leading the horse.

Walking along, he tried to sift things out and decide what to do next. He reached a high spot on the plain, and as he stopped for breath, he saw that the sun was within half an hour of going down. He knew he was in a tight spot. If he walked back to the ranch, with or without the horse, he would get in after dark, and others would have already come in. If he rode the horse, he stood the chance of arriving just as Bridge and the others were riding in or putting their horses away. If he rode like hell, he might be able to get in ahead. Then he would have to decide what to do with the horse and saddle.

He rode like hell. By now he had learned a few different ways to come in off the range, so he went around to the far end of the buildings. Seeing that the others had not come in and left their mounts, he stripped the brown horse and left it in a corral where he didn't think the others would notice it in the dark. He put the saddle and bridle on a rack and left the barn through the back way. When he stepped into the bunkhouse, Pat was still the only man there. He was sitting at the table looking the other way, and he turned around sharp when the back door opened.

"Where the hell have you been?" he asked, a cigarette dancing in his lips.

"Oh, the boss called me over and told me the long story of how he's goin' to bring in a new bride and wants to get the place cleaned up."

Pat finished a puff on his cigarette. "He ought to haul away that trash pile as well."

"That was one of the things he talked about." Ed still didn't know what to think about going into the cellar. It had flitted in and out of his mind for the last couple of hours, and it reminded him of another of Emerson's stories. It concerned a man in Sacramento who was in the habit of picking up old drunks and vagrants and offering them the price of a bottle to go dig a hole to bury trash. Once the victim dug the hole, the man killed him and buried him in it, but not until he did unspeakable things to the man. When the police caught up with him, he had more than a dozen of them buried along the river. Now with Pat's mention of the trash, Ed liked the idea of the cellar even less.

"It's well he should think of it. I've told him about it a few times already." Pat drummed the table top with his fingers. "Those others ought to be comin' in any time."

"The ones from town?"

"Well, them too. But I meant Bridge and the crew."

It was after dark when the men who had been cutting hay filed into the bunkhouse. None of them, including Bridge, seemed in a good mood, but they washed up and took their places as Pat laid out the grub.

A strained atmosphere hung above the supper table as the meal progressed. The other two riders did not come in, and of course Cooley didn't, either. Pat said all three were probably still laid up in a whorehouse.

Bridge, who had finished ahead of the others, had rolled one of his thin, tight cigarettes and was smoking it. He shook his head. "Those other two wandered off the first night. Herm's by himself."

"Unless he's with a girl," said Pat, with a little "heh, heh."

Bridge lowered his cigarette and, with his voice low and steady, directed his words at Pat. "When I said he was by himself, I meant he wasn't with them other two."

"Oh, sure," said Pat. "I understood you."

"He'll be in sooner or later," said Bridge in the same calm tone. "If he's not in by mornin', I'll be surprised."

* * * * *

The moon was up when Ed went to the outhouse at midnight. He opened and closed the door, then ran soft-footed down to the corrals. Cooley's horse, no doubt hungry, came right up to him, and he turned the horse into the corral where the others fed out of a hayrack and had access to a water trough. Then he hurried back to the outhouse, opened and closed the door, and went into the bunkhouse.

He heard the normal sounds of men breathing and snoring. There was no way of knowing whether Bridge was awake, just as there was no way of knowing whether he would really be surprised if Cooley wasn't in by morning. But he had said one thing that was dead certain. Herm Cooley was by himself.

Chapter Ten

The cook's noises in the kitchen woke Ed as usual, and when he rolled out of bed to get dressed, he saw that Bridge was already seated at the table, wearing his hat and smoking a cigarette. Smoke was gathering around the overhead lamp, which made Ed think it might not be Bridge's first cigarette of the day.

A couple of other hands were getting up as well, so Ed took his time and arrived at the table after they did. In the six weeks he had been working at the King Diamond Ranch, he had tried to remain inconspicuous, so he avoided being alone in Bridge's company or looking straight at him unless Bridge was talking to him. Ed's method seemed to work all right, as the foreman paid him very little attention. This morning Bridge was sitting in his habitual place at the end of the table and facing the front door, so Ed took a seat across from him and down a couple of spaces.

Bridge had his usual restrained air about him, more non-committal than nonchalant, and if anything, he seemed more tense. Pat was standing in a slouch at the end of the table, glancing over his shoulder at the two skillets sizzling on the stove.

The puncher sitting at the end of the table, across from Bridge, asked if anything was new. Bridge did not answer but merely moved his head half an inch up and an inch to the side, as if he were trying to get a better view through the haze.

Pat answered, "Herm's horse is in the corral, and his saddle is in the barn. But he's nowhere around, least nowhere to be seen at this hour. Come daylight, maybe you'll find him passed out on the other side of the harness shed. Bridge says there's no point in gettin' worried."

All three punchers, Ed included, looked at Bridge. He waited a few seconds, as if to emphasize the importance of his opinion, and then he spoke.

"Me 'n' Herm's got an agreement. I don't worry about him, and he don't worry about me."

The first puncher glanced at the foreman's hat and said, "You've been down to the barn already this mornin', then."

"Yeh." Bridge took a pull off of his thin cigarette and added to the sparse cloud around him. In spite of the gentlemanly agreement with Herm, it was apparent that he had some concern and was trying not to show it. The dark, close-set eyes were restless, and they returned time and again to the front door. The expectation was so convincing that Ed, too, in a detached way, expected Cooley to come through the door.

Pat went to the stove and came back with a pot of coffee, which he set on the table. He went back to the stove to tend to the crackling skillets. The man at the end of the table poured four cups of coffee, serving Bridge first. The smell of the coffee mixed with the drifting aroma of fried bacon, and the atmosphere in the bunkhouse began to seem normal.

"Smells like grub," said another hired hand as he took a seat on Bridge's left.

"Comin' up," Pat said over his shoulder. "Grab a cup and don't burn your tongue."

During breakfast, Ed caught a couple more glimpses of Bridge. The man's face lay in shadow, the upper half shaded by the hatbrim and the lower half darkened by a day or two of stubble. The black neckerchief and leather vest looked ageless as ever, and in their flat tone and texture, they complemented the tense, expressionless face and the beady eyes that seemed not to take in anything in particular.

After the meal and another brooding cigarette, Bridge stood up. "We'll all go back and cut hay," he said. "I'll be down at the barn." His roving eyes rested on Ed. "That means you, too."

Ed cleared his throat. "I don't know if you've talked to Mort, but he said he wanted me to do some cleaning up."

Bridge frowned. "What kind?"

"Burn a bunch of papers and some old broken chairs, and I think he wanted me to haul away some rubbish."

After a quick, impatient breath, the foreman's chest settled. "He told you that?"

"Last night. He said he had a new bride comin' in, and he wanted to get things cleaned up."

"Oh, that." Bridge gave a slight toss of the head.

"Well, if you want, I can put it off till later and go along with the rest of you. You could leave him a note. I don't suppose he's up yet."

"I don't leave notes."

"Sorry. I'm just tryin' to do what I'm told. When he hired me, he said to do whatever you told me to, unless he told me different. I'm just not sure where I am."

"You're irritatin' me, that's what. I'm tryin' to get some work done."

For once, Ed was able to play the silent game with Bridge, who was usually the master of it.

"Oh, to hell with it," said the foreman. "You stay here, help Pat with the dishes and all, and when it's good daylight you can hitch up the horses and bring the wagon around. You can do that, can't you?"

"Oh, yeah. I've hitched 'em before, remember."

Bridge did not answer him. He looked at Pat, nodded, and walked out of the bunkhouse.

Pat did not make any small talk as the two of them cleaned up after breakfast. When the task was done and the cook sat down to smoke a cigarette, Ed put on his hat and went down to the barn.

The sun had come up by the time he had the horses hitched and the wagon pulled out into the yard. He wanted to get started loading the rubbish right away so he could put off burning the papers and doing whatever that job entailed. Also, he had a good idea of where he wanted to dump the rubbish.

He went into the barn for a pitchfork and a shovel. Cooley's saddle was where Ed had left it, and everything else seemed calm and in order.

Out in the sunlit morning again, he drove the wagon around the far end of the bunkhouse and back toward the heap. He squeezed the wagon between the corner of the bunkhouse and the pile of trash, where he would be able to toss everything up and to his right. He set the brake, climbed down, and went to work.

If it had just been bottles and cans, wire, and old boots, he wouldn't have struggled much. But mixed in with the loose items were layered masses of old, half-rotted material— pasteboard, newspapers, a folded throw rug, crumpled gunny sacks, and an old tick mattress. Some of the garbage was so unwieldy it slipped off the shovel, while some pieces stuck on the pitchfork tines and had to be scraped off.

The sun warmed his back, and he sweated from the forehead as well as under his shirt. Pat came out the back door twice, stood in the shade of the building, and went in without saying anything.

All this time, Ed expected Ramsey to appear and give his appraisal. At another level, he expected Bridge to ride up behind him.

At last he had the whole pile into the wagon, with the most unhealthy, decomposed matter piled on top of the load. As he was setting the tools inside the tailgate, Ramsey came around from the front of the ranch house.

He was wearing his cattleman's hat and a matching jacket, as if he was on his way to a Stockgrowers Association meeting. His dress for the day also included his vest, silver watch chain, inlaid gunbelt, and ivory-handled revolver. In spite of his groomed appearance and the freshness of the morning, however, his veined face looked as turgid as before.

Reaching into the inside pocket of the jacket, he brought out an oxblood leather case. His diamond ring sparkled as he opened the case and took out a tailor-made cigarette, then struck a match and lit it. As he blew away the smoke, he fixed his hard blue eyes on the hired man.

"I wanted you to burn that other stuff first," he said. "Then you could haul the ashes away, too."

"Bridge told me to go ahead and do this. But those ashes won't be any trouble. I can either bury 'em or scatter 'em."

Ramsey looked around the yard as he took another drag on his tailor-made. "Everyone else is gone?"

Ed felt a prickly sensation, but he tried to keep his voice light and cheery. "Except Pat, of course. And there's a couple of punchers that haven't come back from town yet. I wouldn't be surprised if they come trailin' in, any time now."

"Went on a drunk, probably. Wonder why they can't hold down a job."

Ed walked around the far side of the wagon and pulled himself up to the driver's seat. "Well, these horses have been standin' here a while, so I think I'd better let 'em step out. I won't be long, though, and we'll get that stuff burned."

"You know where you're goin'?"

"Oh, yeah." Ed turned down the corners of his mouth and nodded. "Out to the north. I've got a coulee in mind." He glanced at the heap. "It'll be good and out of sight."

Ramsey's eyes traveled over the load and rested on Ed. "Well, if I don't see you when you get back, come and knock on the door."

"I will." Ed released the brake, untied the reins and separated them, and wheeled out of the space between the two buildings. In another minute, he was driving on the road leading from the ranch yard, and now that he was out in the open, he felt better. He made himself not look back as the horses took on the gradual climb on the trail north.

Not quite at the top of the rise, the road curved around toward the east, passing through the tall brush where Cooley had come into view the afternoon before. Ed turned the team to the northwest, across the unmarked grassland. He thought he would like to get this rubbish into the crevice as soon as possible, but he was in no hurry to return to the ranch house.

The wagon lurched and bounced as it rolled across the uneven ground, and Ed looked back every couple of minutes to see that he wasn't spilling any of the load. The last time he turned around, he saw an image that put a jolt through his whole upper body. Bridge was riding his way on a black horse.

Ed tried to calm himself down and still his shaking hands. No need to stop, he told himself, and certainly no point in going faster. His heart kept thumping, but he did not turn his head until Bridge came riding up on his left.

"You just now headin' out with this?" Bridge's voice was calm and level but loud enough to carry over the creaking and jostling of the wagon.

Ed pulled the horses to a stop. "I went ahead and helped Pat like you told me. Then I had to hitch up by myself. After that I had to load all this mess. All kinds of rotten junk fallin' apart on me." Ed peered over the front of the wagon between the two horses. "On top of that, this thing's jerkin' and joltin' like it's gonna come apart underneath."

"Might be the linchpin." Bridge had stopped his horse and sat with his left hand on the saddle horn and his right hanging loose, not far from the black handle of his pistol. He was not wearing his riding gloves. The sun at his back put his face in shade, so that the rider with his black hat, neckerchief, and vest and the horse with its black coat had the appearance of a large silhouette.

"I heard of one of those that broke, and the horses took off. The wagon tipped over and broke the man's neck."

"You hear a lot."

Bridge did not seem to have improved his humor since early morning, but Ed proceeded as he had done with Ramsey, trying to stay light and casual. Putting on a smile, he looked at the foreman and said, "Did you come to help me unload?"

"Not quite."

Ed shrugged and waited for Bridge to speak again.

"I came out to see what you're doin'." Bridge's voice came in measured syllables. "And to see if you know anything about Herm."

"Not as much as you do."

"How's that?"

"I haven't known him that long."

"You know what I mean—whether you know anything about when he came in or where he is."

"That's what I meant, too. You know him a lot better, so I'd think you'd have a better idea of what he's up to."

Bridge's chest went up and down as he took a breath through his nose. "Pat said you were out for a long while yesterday just before dark and maybe you saw him come in."

"I was talkin' to Mort, or more like listenin' to him."

"Well, I'm just goin' on what Pat said. You might have seen Herm come in."

Ed shook his head. "You said he wasn't in yet when you-all came in at dark."

"I didn't see where he had."

"Well, I don't know. I was inside by then."

Bridge took a few seconds to answer. "When you get done with this, I want you to help find him."

Ed widened his eyes. "I wouldn't know where to look. You don't think he slept in the big house, do you?"

An expression of impatience crossed Bridge's face. "You act pretty stupid, you know, and sometimes I wonder if you know more than you let on."

"Well, it does seem that some people, not least of 'em you and Herm, treat me like I'm dumber than I am. But as for when he came in or where he is now, you can search me."

Bridge gave him a close look, then glanced at the load of rubbish "Go get rid of this, and don't waste any time."

"All right." Ed took up the reins but did not shake them. "By the way, how much do you know about these linchpins and king bolts?" He looked down past his feet as before.

"No more than the next fella, I guess. Just take it slow." Then, as if he didn't like what he had just said, he asked, "Is it all worn and loose?"

"I don't know. From what I can see it doesn't look bad, but when we get goin', it shakes like hell. I don't want it to come apart on me. If it looks all right to you, though, I'll flog these horses."

Bridge gave a heave of impatience, and as he swung down from the black horse, he said, "You're as bad as the rest of 'em. Let me take a look."

Ed climbed down from the wagon and stood aside, taking the reins as the foreman handed them to him. With his right hand on the frame of the wagon, Bridge leaned forward.

"I can't see anything wrong with it. Are you sure—?"

His words were cut short when Ed stuck a pistol barrel into the back of the black vest and clicked the hammer.

Ed, having dropped the reins, reached across with his left hand to pull out the man's pistol. Then stepping back with both guns trained on Bridge's middle, he said, "Now turn around, and don't try anything. Either of these guns could blow a big hole in you."

Bridge did as he was told. He threw a hard, narrow look at Ed and said, "I don't know what you think you're up to."

Ed clicked the revolver in his left hand. "It's my turn to ask questions."

The man in black raised his chin. "You're over-reachin' yourself here, kid, and you're goin' to be sorry."

"Don't count on it."

"Tell me what you think you're up to, then."

"I'll tell you what I want to tell you."

"Give me that gun and quit foolin' around. I don't like someone pointin' a gun at me."

Ed shook his head. "You don't tell me. I tell you."

Bridge gave his hardest look. "I thought somethin' was fishy when Herm didn't show up. Where is he?"

"We're not talkin' about Herm Cooley right now. And we might not get around to it."

"What's that supposed to mean?"

"Could mean a few things."

"Kid, you're goin' to be in deeper than you think if you don't quit foolin' around. I'm startin' to lose my patience."

Ed waved his right pistol. "Call me kid all you want, but we're goin' to answer my questions."

Bridge kept up with his hard look and moved his head from side to side.

"About Jake Bishop."

Bridge's face lost all its tenseness, and then the searching look came back into the close-set eyes. "Who are you?"

"Let's just say it's my turn to be the stranger who comes to call."

Now came a frown and a wince as Bridge tried to make him out. "You're the little kid."

"Doesn't matter."

"By God, I've should've taken care of you, too. I thought of it."

"Back to the question. I want to know why you killed Jake Bishop."

"You'll be a long time findin' out."

Ed raised his eyebrows. "I can be impatient too, Bridge. Don't take anything for granted."

"Pah."

"I'm going to give you another chance to answer. Why did you kill Jake Bishop?"

"Oh, piss on you."

"Was it something you had against him, or did someone else send you? Just doin' your job?"

Bridge's voice came in measured syllables again. "A puky little kid. And it comes to this."

"Don't think I'm afraid to pull the trigger, Bridge."

"You wouldn't talk about it if you weren't—" Bridge lunged forward, his left arm across and palm outward, as if it would stop a bullet.

Ed pulled the trigger, and the shot went in below Bridge's arm and through the buttoned leather vest, next to the top buttonhole.

Bridge fell backward and was spun sideways by the wagon as the team of horses bolted. The saddle horse squealed and took off in a pounding run to the west.

Ed took careful steps toward the body squirming on the ground. He put away his own pistol and shifted the black-handled Colt to his right hand. The wounded man writhed like a snake, and Ed recalled the common saying that a dead snake would twist and turn until sundown. Not this one. He lined up the sights on the spot between the two eyes, which were closed now, and he said, "This is for Jake Bishop."

The eyes opened, the snake eyes of the ancient assassin, and then they went blank as the body went still. There was no need for a second shot.

Ed's mouth was dry and his hands were shaking as he looked up and around. No one was in sight, but he was glad he hadn't had to fire a second shot. To someone listening, two shots were a lot easier to place than one was.

For a moment as he stood in the silence, Ed fought down the panicky feeling that everything had fallen apart. He knew he had to pick up the pieces, but first he had to pull himself together. First of that was to get his wind back. He walked around in a ten-foot circle, bringing his head up and taking deep breaths, stopping to bend over and put his hands on his knees, then walking again, from time to time looking over at the slumped body. All right, he told himself, it wasn't going to be as hard as yesterday, but this one was bloodier and he couldn't be wrestling with it. It was just a dead body, and he needed to get rid of it. He wasn't that far from the spot where he had stashed the first one. He could drag this one the whole way, dump it in, and throw the load of rubbish on top of both. That was a plan.

But he couldn't steady himself. This was the biggest thing he had ever done. Enormous. A cold, calculating killer like Bridge, a man who feared no one and was sure he would always come out on top—and Ed had taken him by surprise and made him pay. That was big, too big to think of now. He had to get rid of the body. Focus on that. Unload the wagon, drive back to the barn, and get the hell away from the King Diamond Ranch. In no way was he going to go down into Ramsey's cellar now. He was done with this place, done with this snake of a killer—no, he wasn't done with anything yet. He needed to catch that black horse, then each thing in its turn.

Time and again he walked up on the horse, and when he was within twenty yards, the horse would flinch and run away. Ed circled around, he approached it head on, he fixed his eyes on the front left shoulder. At last the trailing reins came into his hand. Still shaking, he wasn't sure of himself on horseback, so he walked the horse all the way back to the spot where Bridge lay in the dirt with his hat a few yards away.

Ed followed the same method as the day before, taking the rope from the saddle and hitching up the drag. Holding the reins in one hand and the tail of the dallied rope in the other, he walked sideways and backwards until he had the body on the brink of the draw where the crevice gaped below. Cooley's coulee, he thought, and he rolled Bridge in. He tossed the hat and six-gun in on top.

After that, and fetching the wagon, he had the hard, sweaty work of unloading all the rubbish. The troublesome chunks and pieces presented a nuisance again, as it was all a mixed heap. Using now the shovel and now the pitchfork, he finally got the wagon unloaded and the bodies buried beneath a pile of garbage that anyone would have a hard time digging out.

The sun overhead had passed the noon position, and he had a great hunger as well as a thirst. But he still needed to tend to things.

By now he had decided to strip Bridge's horse and turn it loose. First he would ride it to the tall brush farther east, where he would throw off the saddle, blankets, and bridle. He would lead the horse back here, turn it loose, and drive the wagon to the ranch. All that would take time, but it would leave the least tracks.

* * * * *

When he rolled into the yard, dirty and sweaty and all but exhausted, no human life stirred from any of the buildings. After backing the wagon into the shed and unhitching the horses, he rubbed them down and turned them into the corral. He felt once again that he had no time to lose. Ramsey could show up at the barn door at any moment and interrupt his course.

Ed went to the horse trough and pumped himself a long drink. He sloshed water over his face, then rolled up his sleeves and scrubbed his hands and wrists. The trouble was, he still wasn't one hundred percent sure of his next move. If he saddled his horse and ran for it, he would bring suspicion on himself. If he stayed around, he would be sitting on a powder keg. Furthermore, he didn't know how well he could keep his calm. He was still feeling overwhelmed with what an enormous act he had committed when he pulled the trigger on Bridge. He had no regrets, but he couldn't get rid of the shakes.

As he splashed his face a second time, there came a moment of clarity. He had come to the King Diamond Ranch to find out why someone would want to kill Jake Bishop and to find out whether Bridge had done it on his own or was acting for someone else. He hadn't found out any of that, and to boot, he had killed the person who could have told him though likely never would have. He had closed off one main portal to the truth, and the likelihood of getting any information from Ramsey, much less George the brute, was smaller than a pin point. If there was any more information to be had, Ed knew he was going to have to find it through some other channel. Add to that, he had created a state of turmoil here that could break open at any time. No matter what it looked like if he made a break for it, he would be a fool to stick around.

He caught the buckskin and led it into the barn. As he saddled the horse, he was glad the scabbard and rifle were already tied on. He could roll his blankets and grab his warbag in a matter of moments.

When he led the buckskin into the daylight, the ranch yard was still empty. If anyone was looking out from any of the brows of the big house, Ed could not know it. He walked leading the horse until he came to the hitching rail in front of the bunkhouse. He looped the reins over the rail, paused on the stone step, and pushed open the door.

Inside, Pat rose up from his bunk, where he had been snoozing. "What's goin' on?" he asked.

Ed spoke as he rolled his bedding. "I'm pullin' out."

"What for? Don't you like a little hard work?" Pat was sitting slouched on the edge of his bunk. He cleared his throat and spit in a can.

"I haven't minded any of the work I've done." Ed stuffed his jacket into the canvas bag and hefted it. "Thing is, Bridge fired me."

Pat looked up. "The hell. What did you do?"

"Nothin'. He's just had a bug in his ass all day."

"Well, he wasn't in a good mood this mornin', that's for sure. How about your pay? Are you goin' to draw it?"

"We got paid up before we went to town, so it would only be a half day's pay. Maybe I'll come back for it some time."

"Yeah, and maybe the dog'll have kittens."

Ed hoisted the bedroll in one hand and the bag in the other. "I guess that's it. So long, Pat."

The cook twisted his mouth. "So long, kid."

In less than a minute, Ed had his gear tied onto the back of the saddle and was off at a lope in the hot, dry afternoon. His hands were still trembling, and he felt as if he had killed the goose that laid the golden eggs. He was glad to be putting the King Diamond Ranch behind him, yet he thought there was a grain of truth in his saying that he might be back.

Chapter Eleven

Night had fallen by the time Ed rode into Litch. He had not pushed the buckskin very hard, as he had ridden the horse out to the ranch the day before, and he didn't know how much more riding he had ahead of him. He figured he had a day or two until things broke loose at the King Diamond, and he might be traveling a long ways or not at all.

Anyone who knew him would not expect him back in town for a month, so he needed to have a simple story and stick to it. He was in town on business and was going out again as soon as he was done with it.

Meanwhile, he needed to eat. He hadn't had a bite since breakfast, and the manual labor, the encounter with Bridge, and the long ride into town had drained him. As he tied the buckskin to the hitch rack in front of the café, he wondered if anyone would recognize his horse tonight. Then he realized he had better get used to the idea of looking over his shoulder. None of this was going to go away by itself, and the sooner he found answers to his own questions, the better he could decide what course to take next.

He was glad he decided to go to the café before leaving his horse at the stable, for the man and his wife who ran the place were starting to put things up for the night. Ed took a seat where he could see the front door and the sidewalk beyond, where the light fell.

Two bowls of beef stew and a small plate of cold biscuits made him feel much better, but when he went outside to his horse, he felt once again like a fugitive. He decided to walk the few blocks to the stable, so he unwrapped the reins and set out on foot, leading the buckskin and keeping an eye out around him.

After two right turns, he was walking west down the main street. He paused the Rimfire Saloon, which had its front door closed as usual. He wondered who might be standing or sitting inside, and he wondered whether anyone in this town had the information he was looking for—and if so, whether he, Edward Dawes, would be able to get at it.

He put up his horse in the stable, and for an extra two bits, the stable man let him roll out his blankets on a bed of straw. When the man had gone away with his lantern and Ed had gotten nestled in his bed with his six-gun at hand, he felt the night settle in around him. Except for the shift of horses' feet and the sound of animals eating hay, the night was silent. No noise came from the street nor from the Rimfire Saloon fifty yards away.

He let his thoughts jump a great distance, out to a spot in the vast interior country, where lamp lights might still be burning. Maybe the great turmoil would begin tomorrow, when it became evident that Bridge's absence was as mysterious as Cooley's. At the moment, Ed could imagine Pat sitting up late, smoking cigarettes, wondering what was going on. He could imagine Ramsey as well, wondering where in the hell the kid had dumped the garbage, why Bridge had fired him, and why Bridge hadn't come in. Ed hoped that the boss and the cook at the King Diamond figured Bridge was out looking for Cooley. They would assume, as anyone would, that no one would have gotten the best of the hard-case foreman—not on his own range, where he kept a crew of dummies. Sooner or later, though, they would have to change that assumption.

Ed wondered if the other two punchers had come in or whether there were five empty cots in the bunkhouse. He hadn't seen another rider on the way into town, but they might have seen him and gotten out of the way until he rode past. Whatever the case, the bunkhouse would have a tense feeling in the air for whoever was staying there.

Ed made himself think of George the brute. He was part of the layout, too, and nothing to forget about. Ed could picture the brute and his master at daylight, or whatever time they got up, setting out on a search. George would be on the trail like a bloodhound, with Ramsey puffing along in tow.

Enough of the King Diamond Ranch, Ed told himself. He needed to get some sleep. He was in town on business. Before he drifted off, however, he thought of Ravenna. She would understand that he had done what he had to, but he needed to keep her from being dragged into the complications. This was his mess, and he had to work his way out of it himself.

* * * * *

Grey light was filtering into the stable when Ed opened his eyes. He had heard movement, and now he placed it as the stable man going about his morning chores. Ed closed his eyes.

He awoke at the sound of voices. The stable man and someone else were speaking in matter-of-fact tones. Footsteps came down the row of stalls, and someone led a horse away.

Ed could not go back to sleep. At the first sound of voices, he had expected to hear the stable man say, "That's him sleepin' in the straw," and even though the second voice turned out to be just another customer, Ed was past the point of lounging in his bed any more.

Having eaten late and plenty, he was not hungry yet, but it was too early to pay any visits. He went to the café and took his time drinking two cups of coffee. When he walked outside again, the sun had risen high enough that he thought he could knock on Tyrel Flood's door.

The old man's voice bellowed from within, so Ed pushed the door open and looked into the dim interior.

"Come in, come in," the old man said again. "Ain't nobody here but me 'n' the cat."

Ed stepped inside and saw Tyrel sitting at the kitchen table as before, but without the knife stuck in the tabletop. The old man was dressed in his usual sagging clothes and had not yet put on his spectacles.

"Well, hello there," he called, with a tone of surprise. "Are you still in town? I'd thought you'd have left by now."

"I did, but I had to come back. I've got some business to look after."

"So you come to see old Tyrel. Must not be very important. Here, sit down."

Ed crossed the front room, and he took a seat at the table.

"How about some coffee?" asked the host, gathering his stick as if he were about to get up.

"No, thanks. I just had some."

"I don't suppose you need an eye-opener."

Ed laughed. "No, I don't. But thanks again."

"I'll finish eating, then, if you don't mind." Tyrel clacked his spoon into a crockery bowl.

"Go ahead." Ed saw that the bowl held a serving of boiled rice and raisins, the kind of pudding that some people called speckled puppy.

"Tell me what's on your mind, if anything. Not that I want to pry into your business."

"Quite to the contrary. I came to see if I could ask a couple of questions."

"No harm in askin'."

Ed waited a few seconds as he took a breath, and then he began. "Well, you know, I've been workin' out at the King Diamond Ranch, of my own choice, and it always seems that the men in charge there have got somethin' they don't want others to know."

Tyrel looked up, giving a slow stare with his glassy brown eyes in their yellow setting. "That's always the way it is there, from what I understand."

"And it's not just little things, like slappin' a brand on mavericks, though they do some of that, as well as drive in good beef with someone else's brand and put it on the meat hook. They don't hide that from their own hands, at least not from me."

Tyrel swallowed a spoonful of pudding and said, "I don't have any opinion on that."

"Neither do I, or not very much. And like I say, that's not the part I'm wonderin' about. It seems to be somethin' else, somethin' bigger."

"Could well be." Tyrel was cleaning out the bottom of his bowl.

"Here's how it is. They bring in new hands every year, most of 'em men who aren't likely to keep a job or stay in one place anyway. It's as if they don't want anyone to know anything. It seems they even bring in some kind of detective, or man of confidence, to see if anyone is on to anything. All of that, plus they're quick to jump if they think someone is spyin' or snoopin'. They give the idea that they're sittin' on somethin', and it's not a golden egg."

"You might be right." Tyrel pushed his bowl away. "So is that your business? Are you a junior detective?"

"No, I'm not, but I'd like to know what kind of secrets are being protected, if there are any."

"So you come to ask me."

Ed shrugged. "Well, I remember you told me that if I had any questions or wanted to know more about old Snake Eyes or old Ramses, I could ask you."

Tyrel looked at the table and then up. "I don't remember exactly how I put it, but I would have meant opinion more than fact."

After what felt like a setback, Ed summoned up more nerve. "I already knew what you thought of them, at least in a general way, and that is that they're over-bearing and might be crooked."

"That might not be an inaccurate summary."

"But you draw the line at actual information."

The old man did not answer right away. He reached across the table for his pipe and tobacco, then took up the pipe and stuck his yellow, ridged fingernail into it. After a scrape that did not produce much, he looked up and asked, "Have you ever heard of the Dead Hand?"

"Not unless it's a hired man they've got buried in the cellar."

"No, it's an idea. A figure of speech." He scraped again with the thick fingernail, his head lowered so that Ed could see his thin, straggling grey hair and spotted scalp.

"Not like Dead Man's Hand?"

The old man raised his head. "No, it's somethin' else. It's an idea about the past, how it controls the present. When I first heard of it, it was in connection with the dead hand of Shakespeare. The idea was that even when he was long gone, his influence was still around. People weren't free to do something new. They were ruled by the past." Tyrel reached into his trousers pocket and took out the little knife with the handle that looked like whalebone. He opened a blade and started scraping, and in a minute he began to talk again, raising his eyes now and then. "Well, the idea of the Dead Hand isn't just the notion that history won't die, like people still wantin' to argue about secession and all that, you know. It also means things in a person's past that's got a grip on him. Rules his life. That's why they call it the tyranny of the past."

"Secrets, then."

"Sometimes not very secret, but tyrants all the same."

"So if you hire men that don't know much about you, then you don't have as much to deal with."

"Somethin' like that, though you might have at least one person to help keep order, keep all the little beasts from gettin' out."

Ed nodded in slow motion, taking it in. "Then I'm not just dreamin' it up, that there's a secret or two bein' protected."

Tyrel rapped the bowl of the pipe upside-down in his palm and then rubbed his hand on the upper leg of his trousers. "Now we're gettin' back to fact and information instead of opinion or theory." He turned the pipe right-side-up and blew through it.

"Is that something you don't want to talk about, or would prefer not to?"

Tyrel fixed his old eyes on his guest. "I like you, young fella, and I have from the beginning. But I don't know how much good it would do you to know some things. Somethin' flies out at the wrong moment, and Snake Eyes could kill you. Just like that. Or Ramses himself if it came to it." The old man shook his head. "Some things aren't worth it. Better to die in your bed, even if you're just an old drunk with nothin' but a cat to give a damn about you."

"Maybe some things are worth it."

"To you, maybe, if you don't know any better."

"I think the truth is worth it. Worth some risk, anyway."

"Might be, to you. There's some of it out there, probably more than I know. But even with what I do know, I'm not sure I'm the one to tell you. Not at this point, anyway."

Ed gave it a moment's thought. He wished he could tell Tyrel that the threat of Snake Eyes was in the past, but he needed to keep that to himself, and as the old man said, Ramsey himself could do serious harm. So could George the brute. "I don't blame you," he said at last.

"It's none of your worry. But if one person knows somethin', there's probably someone else that does as well."

The old man's stubbled cheek twitched as he poked tobacco into the bowl of the pipe. "How long has it been since you've seen Cam Shepard?" he asked without looking up.

"Since before I went out to work on the ranch."

"He always appreciates a visit. Since you've got nothin' better to do than visit the halt and the infirm, you could go cheer him up. You did a marvel here."

"That's what I like to do. Spread good will wherever I go."

* * * * *

Ravenna was surprised to see Ed, but she was busy at work and didn't have time to chat. She did say, however, that Mr. Shepard had not been feeling well of late and didn't come out of his room until the middle of the day. That left Ed at loose ends, so he went back to the stable to rest and to keep out of the public eye.

He returned to the boarding house to take noon dinner, and after the meal he contrived to strike up a conversation with Cam Shepard. The man looked worse than Ed remembered, as he had a pasty face, swollen and rough-textured, with a bulbous nose that looked as porous as that part of the turkey called the Pope's nose, with the exception that Shepard's nose shaded from scarlet to purple. His eyes were small and bleary, and several of his teeth were missing. His stomach protruded in a shape that should make anyone feel uncomfortable, and his shirt fell away straight down. The shirt fit loose on his shoulders, which looked meager, and his trousers billowed around bony hips and thin legs.

In the presence of such a wreck, Ed tried to act as if everything was normal. "I was talkin' to Tyrel Flood this morning about one thing and another, and he said you might be a person to talk to about a certain topic."

Shepard's eyebrows lifted. "And what topic might that be?"

"Maybe a ruler of ancient Egypt and a beady-eyed individual."

"Oh," said the older man, with a knowing look. "Sometimes I go for a walk this time of day."

"Really?" Ed cast a glance over the wasted physique.

"You bet. I just don't walk fast."

"That would be all right with me. Do you have a hat or a cane?"

"Don't need 'em."

Ed gave the man his shoulder to hang onto as they went down the front steps. When they came to a stop on the sidewalk, Ed asked, "Which way do you like to go?"

"Don't be foolish. Did you or did you not offer to buy me a drink?"

"I suppose I did."

"Then you know which way we're goin'."

The walk seemed to take forever, and Ed felt more than conspicuous, shuffling along in broad daylight with a man who looked as if he had crawled out of a crypt. At last they came to the door of the Rimfire Saloon, where they passed from glaring sunlight to dusky shadows. Ed steered Shepard to a table and helped him to a seat, then took a chair himself about two feet around the curve.

The older man heaved a long sigh. "I don't get out very much," he said, "so I appreciate this."

"It's my pleasure," Ed replied, feeling a bit guilty that he might not be telling the complete truth. All the same, he knew Cam Shepard did appreciate being able to go out and visit the sort of old haunt he used to frequent. Ed had understood, during his stay at the boarding house that winter, that Mr. Shepard drank his liquor in his room while Mrs. Porter pretended not to notice. Sometimes Cam ventured out to visit

Tyrel Flood if there wasn't too much ice on the walkways, but an excursion to a saloon was a rarer event, because of the cost as well as the effort. So even if the present visit was not a complete pleasure for Ed, he didn't mind helping Cam Shepard find his.

At a signal from Cam, the bartender appeared with a bottle of whiskey and two glasses and set them down. As the man went to pour the first glass, Cam said, "Go ahead, Henry, but leave the bottle here for right now."

Ed nodded to the barkeep and pointed to himself, as a way of saying he would take care of the cost. Henry made a bow of the head in return and glided away.

Cam held up his glass. "Well, here's to it, kid, and many thanks."

"You bet." Ed moistened his tongue and upper lip with the liquor and set down his glass.

Cam's throat looked like a horse's when the animal drank upward from a trough. "Ahhh," he said. He licked his lips and set down the glass. "Now, to pick up where we left off."

Ed tipped his head back and forth. Keeping his voice low, he said, "You told me once that you used to work on a ranch where I've been working."

"That's right." Cam closed his eyelids and opened them.

"As you may have guessed, I've had an interest in what you might call the history of one or two of the people out there."

Cam gave a faint nod.

"I went to Tyrel to see what he could tell me. He asked me if I was a junior detective, and I told him I'm not, in the sense that I'm not working for anyone else. My interest is purely personal."

With his face relaxed and his eyes looking dull, Cam gave another dip of the head.

"Tyrel doesn't seem to be interested in talking much about details. For one thing, he says others know more than he does, and for another, he says it's not worth it."

"Probably isn't." Cam had his lips set tight.

Ed took a slow breath to strengthen his own resolve. "If you're dead set against it, I won't try to convince you. But I can tell you why I'm interested. I trust you that it won't go any further, 'cause it has some risk to it as well."

"Sure." Cam raised his eyebrows and took another drink.

Ed moved his chair closer and spoke in as low a voice as he thought he could and still be heard. "It goes like this. About fifteen years ago—no, more like sixteen now, but about the time you would have begun work there, from what you said—this fellow Bridge did something. I was there."

Cam, who seemed to be holding his eyes open with difficulty, said in a muffled voice, "Go on."

"I was a little boy, not quite five years old. He came to the place where I lived, I got sent away for a few minutes, and I heard a gunshot. This man Bridge rode away, and the man who had cared for me like a father was dead in the snow."

Cam's face was cloudy, but he moved his head in agreement.

"Now what I've wanted to know is whether he did it on his own or whether he was working for someone else. It makes a difference, a hell of a big difference, as to what I do next."

With his mouth still set tight, Cam breathed in and out through his nose. He licked his lips, took a drink, and licked again. "You're lookin' to open up a lot of trouble, kid. There's more than one reason a couple of people want to keep it all under cover."

Ed shrugged. "Well, I don't blame you if you'd rather not say anything. If you know someone else I could ask, though, I would appreciate it."

Cam's upper body rose and fell as he breathed through his nose again and made a whistling, wheezing sound. Then he fell to coughing, hawked, and pointed at a spittoon by the bar. Ed fetched it for him, and after the older man spit, he said, "Let me tell you something, kid. I don't expect to live much longer, so in a way I don't care who knows what or who doesn't."

Cam raised his shirt and gave Ed an appalling sight. His belly swelled out tight and round, and beneath the crest of it his navel poked out in an additional excrescence, not unlike the blown-out rear-ends of some hogs and sheep Ed had seen. The difference was that the growth on Shepard's belly was pink and self-contained, not broken open.

Ed widened his eyes and could not find anything to say.

Cam held the underside of his belly as Ed had seen him do before. The man continued speaking. "You see, my guts are all shot to hell. They say it's the liver. They can drain water off this, and then it fills up again. Nothin's worth a damn. I can feel it."

"I'm sorry to know that."

"No reason for anyone else to be sorry. I'm just tellin' you why, in one way, I don't care." He took a breath in and out with his mouth open. "But in another way, if I thought I was just helpin' these other sons of bitches, I might wish I'd said something." Drawing his brows together and lowering his voice, he said, "You haven't mentioned the name of this man that got killed. I think I know who it might have been, and if you don't want to say, I don't want to ask point-blank."

"I was prepared to say, if I thought it would lead me to an answer to my question."

Cam moistened his lips with his tongue. "It could." He motioned with his head as he glanced at the shallow bit of whiskey he had left in his glass. "Pour me some more whiskey if you would."

Ed uncorked the bottle and poured a good three fingers' worth.

The older man nodded and said, "Go ahead."

Ed leaned his head closer and said, "His name was Jake Bishop." He leaned back in his chair.

Cam took a drink and seemed to have to force himself to swallow. With his voice still lowered so that Ed had to lean in to listen, he said, "I thought that was what you would say. And here's what I think I can tell you. You ought to talk to a woman named Leah Corrigan. She lives in Ashton."

Ed nodded as he placed the town in his mind, east of Glenrose. "And can you tell me what part she has in it?"

"She used to be married to Mort Ramsey."

Cam sat back and waved his hand, and Ed understood that the confidential part of the conversation was over. He resumed a normal position in his own chair.

"And that's the last time I got bucked off a horse," said Cam, his voice much louder now.

Ed picked up his drink and took a small sip. The taste made him shudder as it brought back memories of his recent misery with the stuff. "How long did you do that kind of work?" he asked.

"Just five years. I came out west when I was forty-two, worked five years in Thunder Basin, then came to town and went to clerkin'. Did that until a couple of years ago, when I couldn't get around very well any more."

"Oh, I thought maybe you'd been a ranch hand longer than that."

"Nope. And I don't expect to go back to it."

Daylight poured into the saloon as the front door opened. Two men walked in, silhouettes at first until the door closed and Ed recognized the two punchers who had not yet returned to the King Diamond Ranch. The one in front seemed to hesitate when he saw Ed, and then the two of them came over.

"Hello, Tom. Hello, Fred."

The one in front, Tom, did the speaking. "Looks like we're not the only ones late gettin' back. We're just on our way now, stopped in for a snort in case we get bit by a snake on the way. When are you goin' back?"

"Actually, I'm not." After a couple of seconds, Ed added, "Bridge fired me."

"The hell he did. He might fire us, too. But we're ridin' company horses, and we need to go back and get our gear anyway, even if we are fired. Did he say anything about that—about us?"

"Not while I was there."

"Huh. What did he fire you for, or is it something I shouldn't ask?"

"Not at all. He just seemed to get fed up with something, and he told me to scram. You might hear a different story from him, but I don't care. I'm finished there."

"Well, you never know," said Tom. He and Fred nodded to Cam, said "So long" to Ed, and went to the bar.

Cam went through a short coughing spell and expectorated into the spittoon. "I don't think you mentioned that you'd been fired."

"I guess I didn't. But now that I had to leave there, I've had all the more reason to have to get my answers somewhere else."

"I wish you well, kid." Cal glanced at the other two punchers, who were standing down the bar a ways. "Just be careful. That fella Bridge would just as soon put a bullet through you as look at you."

"He may already have wished he did."

Chapter Twelve

When Ravenna finished her evening's work, she suggested that they sit on the back porch so they could be by themselves, but Ed said he didn't want to have to worry about eavesdroppers. He and Ravenna settled on the dining room, and they sat at the far end, away from the kitchen, the door to the sitting room, and the one lit lamp. From the beginning, they spoke in low tones.

"I was surprised to see you in town again," she said. "How soon do you have to go back to the ranch?"

"Well, I don't have to go back. I'm not working' there any more."

"Did you quit?"

"I think that's probably the closest. When I first came to town, the face I put on it was that I was here on business, which is the truth, but it turned out pretty thin by itself. When I ran into a couple of the other punchers, I went ahead and told them what I told the cook, which was that I got fired."

"And that's not what happened?"

"Not exactly. Well, no, not at all. There's quite a bit more to the story, but I think I'd better wait to tell you the rest. For one thing, the less you know, the easier it is for you to stay out of any trouble."

"Are you in trouble, then?"

"I might be pretty soon."

She gave him a studied look. "Does it have anything to do with the fight you got into the other night?"

"With Jeff? No—actually, it might, in the sense that I had some trouble with a fellow who seemed to have heard something from Jeff. But I don't think that's going any further."

"Well, that's good. As I've said before, I don't like him."

"Neither do I, as you can imagine."

She gave a little sigh, then assumed a more energetic tone as she picked up the conversation again. "And your main plan? You were hoping to find out about those two men. I would guess that if you're not working there any more, you either found out everything you needed to know or ran into some trouble."

"I ran into a dead end. I had no question about who had done it, you know, but I got to a point where I could see I wasn't going to get any information as to whether the other one had a hand in it. So I had to pull out and see if I could learn something in some other way."

"So that was the business you came to town on."

"Right. I went to Tyrel Flood and asked him what he knew, and he suggested that I talk to Cam Shepard. So that's what my visit with him was about. He used to work there, you know."

"I think he might have mentioned it. I do know he worked in a store for several years. Poor man, he hasn't had an easy life."

Ed rolled his eyes. "Not from the looks of him."

"Mrs. Porter said he had a fall in life. She never said what kind, just that he had a fall."

"That might have been why he came out west. He said he came out here about fifteen years ago, so he wasn't a youngster looking for adventure and fortune. He said he's fifty-seven, and he was forty-two when he came here. That's a whole life for a lot of men."

"And then to lose it all, or whatever happened. Poor man, it could happen to anyone."

Ed could not imagine it happening to himself, but he did not have a very clear picture of himself at forty-two, either. "Well," he said, "I hope I didn't get him into much harm today. He did enjoy the drinks he had."

"It's good that he can enjoy something, but he's really not well at all."

"That's what he told me." Ed recalled the grotesque image of the man's belly and navel. "Anyway, he had a suggestion of what I could do next."

"Oh, really?" Ravenna seemed to be glad to change the subject also.

"Yes. He told me of another person I could go ask." Ed looked around the room and lowered his voice. "A person I don't know, who lives in a town east of here."

Ravenna nodded.

"I'm not trying to be mysterious, but again, there's some of this that I think it would be just as well if I told you later."

She gave a faint smile. "That's all right. Do you think you'll come back here after that, before you go somewhere else?"

"I think so. It looks like a long day's ride there, maybe a day to ask my questions and lay over, and then a long day's ride back. Something like that. I'd give it three days."

She put her hand on the tabletop and touched his. "Is it the kind of trip that might have trouble in it as well?"

He smiled as he took her hand. "I don't think so. If there's trouble, I think it'll be waitin' for me somewhere else."

"At the ranch."

He tipped his head to each side. "Probably." To himself he said, *Or here in Litch.*

"So do you plan to start out tomorrow?"

"That's right. And I think there's something I should do before I go."

"What's that?"

"I should have done it before, but I didn't think of it." He paused and then went on. "I ought to give someone a detailed description of me and my effects in case anyone would ever need to know it."

"In case—"

"Well, yeah, in case something happened."

"So you want to give this inventory to me?"

"If you don't mind. Do you have a pencil and paper?"

"I can get it. Just a minute." She got up from her chair and came back in less than a minute with a pencil and a sheet of letter-writing paper.

He then gave her a description of himself, his horse, his saddle, his rifle, his pistol, and his pocket knife. "I don't carry a watch or any keys," he said, "or any photographs. I don't have any fillings in my teeth, or any scars or birthmarks."

"No keepsakes?"

He shook his head. "Never had any. I'm used to travelin' light."

She gave him a tender smile. "Would it weight you down very much if I gave you one?"

His heartbeat picked up a little as his eyes met hers. "Do you have a picture of yourself?"

"No. And you say you don't have one of yourself either?"

"Me? Oh, no. But what do you have for me?"

"I can give you a lock of my hair."

His eyes swept over her dark, flowing tresses. "I wouldn't want you to take a gouge out of your beautiful head of hair."

"Don't worry," she said, her dark eyes softening. "I can take some out where it won't be noticeable."

Stranger in Thunder Basin

* * * * *

Long shadows stretched across the open range as Ed rode east from Litch the next morning. The buckskin was stepping out just fine, and Ed felt well equipped with his rifle, rope, pistol, warbag, and bedroll. Although he had a sense of trouble pending and had no knowledge of how things had developed at the King Diamond Ranch, he hoped to be left alone on his present journey. Only Cam Shepard and Ravenna had an idea of where he was headed, and someone would have to squeeze to get information out of either of them.

He rode past the spot where he had crossed trails with Jory and Homer a few days earlier, and beyond that he came to the Barrow. Past the large earth mound, the road ran north to the place where Jory and Homer worked. After his time in Litch and Thunder Basin, his stay at the Tompkins Ranch seemed like an earlier life, much farther back in time than a year ago. Yet he could still picture the massive butte that rose up in back of the ranch headquarters, the two young cottonwoods growing out of the bank of a man-made pond, the swirling black mane of the horse that bucked him off, and Homer singing "Lonesome Jim" in the bunkhouse.

Ed stopped to gaze at the road running north. In spite of the fond memories, the Tompkins Ranch had had its portion of unpleasantness in the presence of Jeff. But he was no longer there, and even when he was, the ranch was as good a place as a working man could hope for. Ed wondered if roads like that were closed to him forever now, after the trouble in Thunder Basin. He would begin to know when he returned to Litch in a couple of days or so. Meanwhile, he had business ahead. Looking through his horse's ears again, he touched a spur to the buckskin's flank and kept riding east.

He passed through Glenrose in the afternoon, when the heat of the sun went through the back of his shirt. The sound of the steam-driven rock crusher pulsed in the hot air. He passed Emerson's blacksmith shop, which stood with the door open but no one visible. Ed recalled his many days in that enclosure—the heat of the forge, the weight of the leather apron, the clumsiness of the heavy gloves. The shower of sparks, the smell of hot metal, the clang of iron on iron.

He looked to the other side and down a cross street, where he remembered a night when he went by himself to a place of dim lights. He recalled the name, Amelia. She had been a kind woman, gentle, and she had known what was good for a boy who needed to know about those things. That incident, also, had a place in his past.

* * * * *

The long shadows were reaching across the ground to the east when Ed rode into the town of Ashton. He calculated that he had ridden more than fifty miles and had been in the saddle for twelve hours, plus rest stops. He had not pushed the horse too hard, but it had been a long day, and the animal could use a rest.

Although Ashton was something of a crossroads town, with the east-west road running on into Nebraska and beyond, its main thoroughfare ran north and south, as it lay along the old Cheyenne-to-Deadwood stage route. Ed knew that riders from Thunder Basin could come to this town if they rode east twenty or thirty miles and then south another forty or so, but the men at the King Diamond Ranch didn't talk much about the place. Furthermore, the two riders who would know that trail were in a ravine together—unless they had been discovered by now.

Ed found a stable two blocks south on the main street. He put up his horse, stowed his gear, and arranged to spend the night. Now on foot, he walked downtown to find something to eat. In a café on the west side of the street, he ate the evening plate special, which consisted of roast beef, mashed potatoes, and gravy. The heavy-boned, deep-eyed woman who took his order said there was rhubarb pie as well. Rhubarb was one thing that grew here, she said. People had apple trees, but it wasn't one year out of three that they got enough apples to make a pie. Ed took her up on the offer and had a slab of pie with green rhubarb filling—sour and not the red he expected, but pie all the same.

After supper, he strolled up the main street a couple of blocks, crossed over, and walked down the other side. He passed a set of batwing doors, where he caught the smell of whiskey and heard the tinkling of a piano and the easy tones of a couple of men's voices. He walked on. Ahead of him, a man stepped up onto the sidewalk. The man wore spurs with large, clinking rowels, the kind that were as big as silver dollars and might have been filed out of a pair. The man blocked the sidewalk, smoothing his mustaches as he looked at himself in a shop window. At the last second, he stepped aside to let Ed go by.

Night was falling by the time Ed returned to the stable. For people in the saloons, it was early; for people on the rangeland, it was time for bed. Ed imagined the ranches around here were like any others—most of them calm, orderly places where men like Jory and Homer lay down without having to bolt the door or put a pistol beneath the pillow. Then his thoughts traveled to the King Diamond Ranch, which might be as roiled up as an anthill that someone had carved at with a shovel. Ed recalled his dream about Cooley and his legion of demons, and now he pictured Ramsey trying to whip his nondescript ranch hands into a frenzy like his own.

All that in its place. Ed was sure he would have to face some of it when he went back. For the present, he needed to get what rest he could, and on the morrow he would find out what kind of a person Leah Corrigan was.

* * * * *

In the morning, Ed lingered over a breakfast of hotcakes and coffee. From his seat by the window, he waited as life began to stir in front of the other businesses along the street. A storekeeper, a pharmacist, a dentist, a lawyer, a jeweler—each in turn opened his door. Those on the east side who had shades raised them. The storekeeper swept the sidewalk in front of his store and set out a barrel of long-handled tools with shovel, rake, and hoe heads standing cheek by jowl with mops and brooms. The dentist stood in front of his door and took out his watch every two or three minutes to look at it. The jeweler set his merchandise in the window, no doubt after it had spent the night in a safe.

When the waitress with the deep-set eyes slowed down as she passed his table, Ed stopped her. Speaking in a soft voice, he said, "Excuse me, but I was wondering if you could help me find someone I came to this town to see."

"I might be able to," she said. "Who is it?"

"A person I've never met. Her name is Leah Corrigan."

The waitress gave him a close look, and not seeming to find an illumination, said, "She lives in the upstairs of Mr. Jensen's house."

"I see. And he is—"

"He's a lawyer. He has his office in the front part of his house right down this same street a couple of blocks, and on your right. A white house with black trim. You'll see his sign."

"Thank you," he said. "I'm obliged."

"Don't mention it. Anyone could tell you the same."

Ed finished his coffee. After leaving a nickel and a dime for a tip, he paid for his meal at the cashbox and walked out onto the sidewalk.

Two blocks down, she said. He had walked right past the house both times when he went from the stable to the downtown area.

As he approached it now, with his eyes open, he saw a house like several others along the west side of the street. It was a two-story frame house, painted white, with a roofed porch. The eaves and window frames were painted black, as was the door frame as it came into view. A sign attached to the wall between the front door and the window on the right had clear lettering, thanks to its being sheltered and probably touched up once a year. The top line read, "Wm. D. Jensen," and the second line, in smaller letters, read "Attorney at Law."

Ed walked up onto the porch and made the brass knocker sound twice. After a minute, he rapped it three more times.

A man opened the door and, giving the visitor a quick look of appraisal, said, "Yes, sir?" He was a neatly dressed man, in a suit and vest and tie, clean-shaven except for a trimmed grey mustache, and well barbered with a head of grey hair thinning on top. He was a little below average height, but he had the air of looking down on others regardless of their own stature, and no less so if they had the cut of a range rider. Ed took him for the man of the premises.

"Are you Mr. Jensen?"

The man gave a slight nod and steadied his blue-grey eyes on Ed. "Yes, I am. How might I help you today?"

"I'm looking for a woman named Leah Corrigan. I understand she lives here."

The man stiffened as he took in a short, measured breath and rested his left hand on the door frame. Ed saw now that he had a pair of wire-rimmed spectacles, which he held by his right side and held out by one stem. In his slight shift in position, Mr. Jensen seemed to be guarding the door. He raised his chin as he spoke.

"I'm sure you won't mind my asking what your business might be with Mrs. Corrigan."

Ed faltered for words that he thought would be adequate. "Well, I'd like to ask a couple of questions about some things that are—well, of personal interest to me. Let me say, personal importance."

Mr. Jensen looked him over again. "Would you mind telling me your name?"

"Not at all. It's Edward Dawes."

The name seemed to mean nothing to the attorney. "Very well, Mr. Dawes. Let me put it this way, and you'll understand I mean nothing personal. But I meet a great many people—mostly men, and mostly older than you—who have a personal interest in other people's personal lives. You understand, I don't shoe horses or sell brooms. Mrs. Corrigan not only lives in proximity, but she also entrusts me to protect her interests, such as they are."

"I understand."

"And if you were to be a little more forthcoming about the nature of your interest, I might more easily form an opinion about the advisability of Mrs. Corrigan listening to you. By the way, where are you from?"

"I came over from Litch."

"Hot weather for traveling."

"Yes, it is."

The blue-grey eyes narrowed in on him. "And what do you want to talk to her about?"

"Well, I understand that at one time she was married to a man who now has a ranch in Thunder Basin."

"That's an unfortunate truth. But it was many years ago, and Mrs. Corrigan has long been free of any legal obligations there."

"No doubt for the best. And I don't want to ask her about anything she might have had to do with him. I'm interested in something he might have done. I've asked a couple of other people, and they have referred me to her. At least the last one did."

"His name? Or hers, as it might be."

"His. A man named Cam Shepard. I have no idea if she knows him or has ever heard of him."

"Nor do I. Wait here." Mr. Jensen closed the door, and Ed heard footsteps leading away.

Several minutes passed, and Ed began to feel the trickle of sweat as he stood in the sunlight. The shade from the roof of the porch reached only to the top of the windows. At least the dentist who had been looking at his watch had shade to stand in.

The door opened, and Mr. Jensen appeared. "Come in," he said. "Have a seat and wait." He showed Ed into a small waiting room with four straight-backed oak chairs, then crossed the room and opened a door, which he left open as he passed through.

Beyond the doorway, Ed could see bookshelves and the front of a varnished desk. He assumed the lawyer left the door open in order to hear the front door as well as to overhear anything that went on in the waiting area.

Ed sat in the room for a good ten minutes, hearing the occasional rustle of paper or clearing of the throat. At last he heard a door open from within, and his pulse quickened as he heard a woman's voice answered by Mr. Jensen's. A few seconds later, a woman came through the doorway. She wore a light blue dress with white cuffs, puffed sleeves and shoulders, and a straight, three-button collar that was closed. Ed stood up with his hat in his hand.

His first impression of her was that she was an unlikely match for Mort Ramsey. Ed would guess her age as forty-five, a good five years younger than the ex-husband. She was of medium height for a woman, with a high bosom, full lips, and a waist that was no longer flat. She had dark blond hair and hazel eyes, somewhere between grey and green. Her face was tan and a little weathered, and her hair seemed brushed back by nature, as if she was not a stranger to the sun and wind. Her eyes had a faraway cast to them, like the eyes of a person who had kept a lookout from a hilltop or a seaside cliff, and he sensed at once that her face would be hard to read. Overall, however, it was more an air she had about her than anything physical that made her seem so unrelated to the man of Thunder Basin.

"I'm Mrs. Corrigan," she said, keeping her hands together in front of her waist. "Please sit down." She moved toward a chair about four feet from his.

"Thank you." When he was seated, he said, "My name is Edward Dawes, and I've come over from Litch. I'd like to thank you for talking to me." Then, remembering Mr. Jensen's choice of words, he said, "Or at least listening to me."

She flicked her eyebrows. "As you can imagine, I don't speak very freely with strangers from off the street. But Mr. Jensen said you were sent by Cam Shepard. I have a faint memory of him, but I remember him as an honest sort. He's well, I hope."

"Not as well as some. He's fallen into poor health, I'm afraid."

Her eyes did not show much expression as she said, "I'm sorry to hear that." She adjusted her hands in her lap and said, "But that's not what you came to talk about."

"No, it isn't. As Mr. Jensen probably told you, I came to ask about something that you might know about—something that might have happened when you were with—um, when you were married to—"

"Mort Ramsey."

"Yes. I'm sorry. I'm not sure how much to—"

"Oh, I can choke out his name without having a seizure." An impassive expression, beyond bitterness, seemed to have settled upon her face.

"Anyway, there was something that happened about fifteen, sixteen years ago, something crooked, and I'm wondering if he might have had a hand in it."

"If it's crooked, he might well have. If you know him at all, you won't be surprised at my saying that."

Ed shook his head. "I'm not surprised."

"But as for details, or my opinion of whatever it was, I would prefer not to go into it. That man has no claim on me, and I have no interest in him, his affairs, or anything that others might have against him." Her earlier impression had hardened into something like a stone wall.

"I'm sorry you're so set against talkin' about it," he said. "It wasn't just any old crooked deal."

She held him with her greyish-green eyes, and he was sure she had an inkling of what he wanted to ask about, but he could see they were at a deadlock. But she did grant him another exchange.

"I fought long and hard to get myself disentangled from that man. It wasn't easy. But now that I've got him and everything that pertains to him shut out of my life, I want to keep it that way. I'm afraid, then, that I don't have much more to say."

"I can appreciate that, ma'am. And I'm sorry if I said anything to make you uncomfortable." He rose with his hat in his hand. "Thank you for hearing me out, and I wish you all the best."

Her eyes glanced up at him. "I wish the same to you."

He gave her a bow of the head and turned away, feeling her eyes upon him as he walked out the door. The sun nearly blinded him until he put on his hat, and as he walked down the steps, he realized he was back out on the street much sooner than he expected.

Heaving a long sigh as he stood alone, he thought he would make the best of his visit to this town anyway. He walked back to the two-block area where most of the businesses were located, and he found the jeweler's across from the café.

The proprietor rubbed his hands together and looked forward with a smile as Ed came through the door and tinkled the bell.

"Yes, sir."

"I think I'd like to buy something special."

"Oh, indeed. We specialize in that. For yourself, or someone else?"

"Someone else. A lady."

The proprietor's eyes went up. "Very good, very good. Young lady? Older lady?"

"Young lady." Ed smiled. "Something to surprise her."

The jeweler pursed his lips. "Are you, shall we say, approaching an understanding with the young lady?"

Ed drew his brows together. "Not quite."

"I see. Maybe something more like a tender friendship, perhaps with hopes."

Ed thought of the kiss when Ravenna gave him the lock of hair. "That's probably close."

"Well, then, let us think of a stone. Do you have in mind a brooch, or a set of earrings, or perhaps a ring?"

Ed's eyes lit on a deep red object in the glass showcase. "What's this?"

"That's a ring, of course. A garnet. Set in gold. A beautiful gift for any young lady. And over here we have—"

"I like this one."

"The garnet."

"Yes. Can I see it?"

"Of course." The jeweler reached down into the case, took out the ring, and set it on top of the glass. "I don't suppose you have her finger size."

"Well, no." Ed picked up the ring and looked it over. He thought it was the perfect color. "I think I'll take it."

"Are you sure? We have other—"

"I know what I want when I see it."

The shopkeeper nodded. "Of course. Now back to the finger size. What's she like? Big? Little?"

"I think she's average size."

"Are her hands smaller than yours?"

"Oh, I'd say so."

"Well, here's how to do it, and we can always re-fit this later. If it goes on your little finger, it will probably fit on her ring finger, unless she's a big girl, or she puts on weight—"

"Like I said, she's average."

"That's fine. And see? It goes onto your finger just right."

"I'll take it, then."

"Perfect. And like I said, we can re-size it later if need be."

"She lives a ways off."

"Oh, they can size it anywhere. Wrap it for you?"

"Sure. And what's the cost today?" Ed reached into his pocket.

"Oh, that ring is usually priced at twenty-two dollars, but in the interests of young love, I'll bring it down to twenty. It's a beautiful gift. I'm sure she'll love it."

Chapter Thirteen

As he walked from the jewelry shop to the stable, Ed kept to the east side of the street, not only for the shade but also to avoid passing by the front door of Wm. D. Jensen, Attorney at Law. From the moment he had walked out that door, Ed had been pushing away an empty, sinking feeling that he had achieved very little after coming so far.

He avoided looking in that direction, and when he heard a sound from across the street, he ignored it. The sound came again, and he had a sense that it was being directed at him. When he turned, he saw that he was straight across the street from the house and that Mr. Jensen was standing in the doorway calling to him.

He kept walking, and the man called again. This time when Ed looked across, the lawyer motioned with his arm. Ed changed his course and went over to see what the man wanted.

Pausing at the sidewalk, he gave Mr. Jensen an inquisitive look and called out, "What is it?"

"Come on up here," said the lawyer. "I've got a couple of words to convey to you, and I don't want to shout them into the street."

Ed crossed the small front yard of dry grass and went up the steps. As the lawyer now seemed to be waiting on him, he said, "Well, go ahead."

"Just a few words," Mr. Jensen began. "As you might imagine, Mrs. Corrigan was somewhat disturbed by your visit."

Ed shrugged. "I'm sorry for any of that, and I told her so."

"Perhaps you don't get my meaning, or I don't make myself clear. She was upset."

"Well, I was disappointed. I came quite a ways, and I'm leaving with very little. So even if Mrs. Corrigan doesn't want to tell me anything—and, as I told her, I don't blame her—I'm going to do what I need to do."

"That's just it." The lawyer's voice was firm. "Won't you just let sleeping dogs lie?"

"Like I told you earlier, this is a matter of personal importance to me."

"And you think it isn't to her? Don't you see how inconsiderate it would be if you don't let things be?"

Ed shook his head. "Actually, I don't. What you're suggesting might be convenient for Mrs. Corrigan, but it doesn't work well for me."

The lawyer huffed. "If you won't listen to me, perhaps you'll listen to her."

Ed picked up the word. "I'd be pleased to listen."

"Well, won't you come in, then, and sit down again. I'll see if I can bring her."

After a couple of minutes, Mrs. Corrigan came into the room, wearing the same dress as before and not looking much different as far as her facial expression went. Ed, who was still standing, nodded to her, and at her invitation, the two of them sat down.

Her eyes, grey now, did not stay on him for long but seemed to be watching her hands as she spoke. "I didn't think our earlier conversation ended in a very satisfactory way."

"I felt I came out of it rather short, but I thought that was the way you wanted it, so I left it at that."

She tipped her head to one side but did not look up. "I don't blame you for wanting to know things."

"I'm in a situation where I have to."

"I thought it was something I could keep at a distance, like before, but I can see that—" She held her hand before her eyes and began sobbing.

Ed was surprised to see her break down so soon. He wanted to rise from his chair to comfort her, but he didn't know her well enough, this woman whose way of life seemed so different from his, and whose attorney was just a few feet away. "It's all right, ma'am," he began. "It's something that happened a long time ago. It can't be changed. I was just tryin' to decide what I had to do next."

Now the tears fell. "I don't blame you for resenting any of it."

"Well, I—"

"And I can see that this is a chance to make my peace."

Ed frowned, thinking that they were almost talking at cross purposes, but as she sobbed again, moisture came to his eyes and he felt a lump in his throat. He had not been around women who cried, or any women to speak of. He swallowed and said, "It's good if you can do that."

Her grey eyes, brimming with tears, raised to meet him. "You may have thought I was trying to protect that man, but it was nothing of the sort. I was just trying to protect myself—hide from myself, really. And when it comes to this, I can't. I know it's too late, in more ways than one, to be a mother to you, but I want to say I'm sorry."

The truth washed over him as he sat face to face with the woman whose tears had moved him before he knew who she was. He faltered for words as never before. "Well, I—"

"If you're bitter, or, as I said, resentful, I can't blame you." She dabbed at her eyes with a handkerchief she held crushed in her hand.

Words no longer resisted him. "Not at all. Not toward you. As far as that goes, I haven't had any complaint. Growing up without a mother was just life as I knew it. The people who raised me never said anything about it, and Mrs. Dawes—well, she had her own kids, and I was just someone she and her husband took in to help with the work. But I came through it."

She blinked her eyes and attempted a half-smile. Her cheeks were moist, but tears no longer flowed. "For what it's worth," she began, "I've always had the knowledge, always lived in the shadow of knowing, that I had, um, left a little boy to find his way in the world. It hasn't rested easy with me. Quite to the contrary, it's been a source of lasting guilt, as well it should be. I've never married again—Corrigan is my maiden name—and I've never had any other children." She looked at him with clear eyes.

He nodded.

"The life you see me in now is one of my own choosing. As you have no doubt gathered, I try to retreat from the world. I know I can't hide from the truth, as I indicated a few minutes ago, but with the help of Mr. Jensen, I've thrown up my fortifications and ask that the world leave me alone. In this case, though, I'm glad to make my peace."

"It's more than I expected."

"And like I said, I think it's late in the development of things to try to be the mother I'm not—or failed to be."

Ed felt his eyes moisten again. "Don't be too harsh on yourself." Then his own words surprised him as he said them. "If there's anything to forgive, I do that freely."

"Thank you," she said. "It's very generous of you."

He shrugged. "It's just the way I feel."

"Well, it's a good impulse." Her eyes had a faraway look as they brushed across him. "Maybe it comes from good nature."

"I guess I don't have it in me to hold a grudge against a woman."

"I wouldn't blame you if you did, but it's better in the long run not to cling to bitter feelings if you can keep from doing it." She dabbed at her eyes again with the handkerchief, then sniffed as she raised her head and put on a smile. "That may be a very good place to leave things."

Ed felt a wave of surprise, the faintest swimming of the room around him, and he realized that the big moment of their meeting had passed and he couldn't see a way to go back and fit in other questions. "I guess so," he answered.

She rose from her chair and gave him her hand. "I don't know if we'll ever see each other again. As I said before, I don't see much point in trying to be what I'm not, or haven't been."

"I don't know, either. I want to thank you for being willing to talk to me, though."

"Thank you for your understanding."

In a moment he was out in the sunlight again, realizing once more how little time had lapsed. The knowledge of who Mrs. Corrigan was had swept him over, and he had lost sense of time and purpose. Before he knew it, his time was up and he was out on the street again. He realized he couldn't go back knocking on the door, but he wished he had found a way to ask about Jake Bishop.

That was all right, he told himself. The unspoken agreement was that with as much as she had been willing to tell him, he would not pursue further questions about her ex-husband's doings—at least he would not pursue them with her. But he was sure that he was better armed now than before—better armed, he hoped, and not handcuffed. If Mort Ramsey had ordered the killing of Jake Bishop, then Ed needed to bring him down. Ed had a theory about how and why things might have worked the way they did, but if Leah Corrigan was his mother, Mort Ramsey could, though he hated to think it, be his father. Leah Corrigan had not stated whether the man was or wasn't, and her manner of speaking implied that he wasn't, but it was still a hideous possibility. It gave Ed plenty to brood on for the long ride back to Litch. Not least among his questions was one that did not have a factual answer: how deep did the laws of blood run? How wrong would it be to lift his hand against a man who had that relation with him?

* * * * *

The sun was warm on his back, and it and cast the horse's shadow out front as Ed rode west from Ashton. He was leaving earlier than he expected, but it was late enough in the day that he would not make it to Litch. He passed through Glenrose without giving the town much thought, but when he heard ringing blows from the blacksmith shop, he recalled the triangle made out of an old crowbar.

Past Glenrose, into the afternoon sun, he lapsed into his brooding again and did not come out of it until he recognized the stretch of road leading up to the Barrow, the landmark for the road north to the Tompkins Ranch.

Knowing he could not travel all the way to Litch tonight, and thinking he could cover the twelve miles north before darkness fell, he decided to go that way. The boys would put him up for the night, and he could keep his ears open for any news that might have come down from Thunder Basin.

Supper was on the table in the bunkhouse when Ed walked in. Reuben, Jory, and Homer all showed surprise and insisted he "sit down and grab a spoon." The other four hands, all unknown to Ed, nodded at the introduction and went on eating stew.

Ed remained standing by the door as Reuben got up to go to the kitchen.

"You'd better stay the night," said Homer. "I 'magine you already know that. If you want, you can put your horse away while Reuben scrapes the bottom of the pot."

"That sounds fine." Ed knew the routine well enough, and within ten minutes he was back in the bunkhouse, setting his bag and bedroll on a cot.

"What news?" asked Jory, as Ed settled into his seat.

"Oh, not much. I don't know what you've heard, but I'm not workin' up in Thunder Basin any more."

"Hadn't heard that."

Ed paused before digging into his stew. "Not much to tell. I had a disagreement with Bridge, so I wore out my welcome."

"No one has lasted there very long," Homer put in. "Except Bridge and that other one."

"Cooley."

"Yeah, him."

The table went quiet as the others let Ed eat his supper. The four new hands drifted to their bunks. Jory brushed off the table with his hand, as if he was getting ready for a game of cards or dominoes.

"Have you got another place in mind?" asked Homer. "Or are you just lookin?"

"You could say I'm just lookin'. Askin' around. I had to go over to the other side of Glenrose, and now I'm on my way back to Litch. Thought I'd stop in."

"Glad you did." Homer took out the makin's and went about rolling a cigarette. He paused and made a small gesture toward Jory, who spoke next.

"Mutual friend of ours dropped by. Asked for you."

Ed rested his spoon. "Someone from Arkansas?"

"Yep."

"I wonder what he wanted."

"He didn't say. You know how he is, though. All smiles and best of friends."

"He and I aren't exactly on good terms right now. We had a little set-to the other day. I doubt that he mentioned it."

"No, not at all."

"When did he come by?" Ed went back to eating his stew.

"Just earlier this afternoon. If we'd known you were comin' by, we could have told him to wait." Jory showed his smile.

"I can get by for a while longer without seeing him. On the other hand, I wonder why he's lookin' for me."

"Maybe he knows you're not workin' out there any more, and he wants to offer you a job."

"That would be just about it."

* * * * *

Ed rode into Litch in the early afternoon. The place looked as slow and uneventful as ever. A couple of horses stood hipshot in front of the Rimfire Saloon, a ranch wagon was pulled alongside the Mercantile, and a buggy was just pulling away from the butcher shop. The shadows had not begun to move much, and the population was keeping to indoors in the heat of the day.

Ed watered the buckskin at a trough in front of the livery stable and put him up inside, where he could have oats and a rest. Walking to the west in order to avoid going past the saloon, he traveled the few blocks to Tyrel Flood's shack.

When he knocked on the door this time, the old man himself opened it, looking both disheveled and fierce. His brown-and-yellow eyes glared through the spectacles. "You'd better come in," he said.

Ed crossed into the living room. "What's happened?"

"They've beat the hell out of Cam Shepard, that's what." Tyrel tapped his way back to his wooden armchair and sat down.

"Who has?" Ed stayed on his feet in the middle of the room.

"He's not talkin' at all, but it seems as if it was that big lunkhead that works for Ramses."

"My God, that's hardly a fair fight. Was Ramsey there?"

Tyrel gave an angry nod. "Yeah, the son of a bitch. Sit down, won't you?"

As Ed sat in his usual chair, Tyrel lifted his glass and took a drink.

Frowning, Ed resumed the topic. "What would they want to do that for?"

"Damned if I know."

"Where did it happen, and when?"

"Right out here on the street, not a block away, when he was on his way back to supper."

"He'd been here?"

"Yeah, he came over about this time of day, and we had a few drinks."

"Did he ask you about the business I was on?"

"Damn little. For the most part, we just drank and made small talk, throwin' stones at the rest of the world. Then when he left, they came by in a wagon. They stopped him, and the big one beat the hell out of him."

"He didn't say what they wanted?"

"He hasn't said anything. Someone else saw it, and that's how they knew to take him back to his room. Happened just down the street, and I didn't see a damn bit of it."

Ed shook his head. "This doesn't sound good at all, and I might have been the cause of it in a roundabout way."

Tyrel looked at him over the top of the glass. "You want some of this?"

"No, thanks."

"Then go ahead."

"Well, after I talked to you the other day, I went to see him like you suggested. A little later that day we went to the saloon, and we talked about what I had on my mind. We didn't talk about it very much. But the bartender was there, and a couple of riders who were late gettin' back to work at the King Diamond came in. Either those two or the barkeep could have said somethin' about him talkin' to me."

"Is that somethin' to beat a man halfway to death for? A poor old drunk that can't fight back? Why didn't they wait for you to get back, and give it to you? Not that I'd want 'em to, but that would be more like a man."

"Oh, I agree. But they weren't expectin' me back. Not to the ranch."

Tyrel stared at him. "Did you get fired?"

"That's what I told the cook, and that's what I told the two boys when I saw 'em in the saloon, but the truth is I left there because I had it out with Bridge."

"Had it out. In what way?"

"Well, let's just say he won't ever be able to contradict me on any of it."

Tyrel pursed his lips. "Son of a bitch. So they must have found him, and come after you."

Ed moved his head up and down in slow motion. "Must have."

Tyrel stared off into empty space for a minute before he spoke. "Then where in the hell have you been all this time?"

Ed paused. "It's a little bit of a story. You might want to fill your glass."

"I can fill it any time. Go ahead."

"Well, Cam gave me the name of a woman who used to be married to Ramsey. Lives over in Ashton."

"I've heard there had been a wife, but I didn't know who she was or where she lived."

"By the way, when I was out at the ranch, he talked about bringing a new bride there. Do you know anything about that?"

Tyrel blew out a puff of air. "He's been sayin' that for so long, he must have got to believin' it himself."

"Huh. I wondered. Anyway, back to the story. I went over to Ashton to talk to this woman. That's where I've been for two and a half days, most of it travel."

The old man shifted in his seat. "And what did you find out? Or is it fair of me to ask?"

"I don't mind." Ed paused again, thinking how he wanted to proceed. "At first, she didn't want to talk about details any more than anyone else—meanin' you and Cam, and meanin' no offense."

"That's all right. Go ahead."

"She said she was done with him long ago, and she didn't want to talk about anything."

"Can't blame her." Tyrel waited, and after a minute he said, "And then what? You said 'At first.' I'm guessin' she went ahead and told you somethin'."

Ed sat up straight. "Well, she did. But I think that if I go ahead and tell you, I deserve to hear what you know."

"I tell you, you tell me."

"That's right."

"Well, it sounds like the fat's in the fire, from what happened to Cam and at the ranch before that. So go on."

"She told me she was my mother."

"Son of a bitch." Tyrel opened his eyes and hung his head forward as he gulped. "She told you that?"

"Actually, I think she thought I already knew, and she thought that was why I was lookin' her up."

"That must have been a long ordeal."

"You'd think so, but it wasn't. She wanted to have her say, which was that she was sorry, but she didn't want to go into any of it. So I ended comin' back with more questions than I started out with."

"How many did you have to begin with?"

"One. I wanted to know whether Mort Ramsey had anything to do with Bridge killing Jake Bishop."

"So it was Bridge. I thought so all along. And you did for him." Tyrel gave him a full look. "You've got a lot of guts, kid."

"It seemed like the only way out."

Tyrel sniffed. "And she didn't answer your question."

"I didn't quite get around to it."

Tyrel's gaze went off and away, and it came back. "And what was the new question you picked up?"

"There's either one or more, dependin' on the answer to the first of 'em."

"And that is . . . ?"

Ed had to force himself to say it. "I need to find out if Mort Ramsey is my father."

"I think I will have another drink." Tyrel grabbed the bottle and poured a good three fingers into the tumbler. "Want some now?"

"No, thanks. The smell of it still reminds me of how sick I got last week." Ed waited what he thought was a respectable interval for the old man to answer, and when he didn't, Ed spoke again. "So that's what I found out, and those are my questions."

"I know, kid. I'm just thinkin' of where I want to start. And I don't know how much of this you're gonna enjoy hearin'."

"I'm not in this for the enjoyment at this point."

"Damn good thing." Tyrel raised his eyebrow and took a drink. After a wince and a shudder, he said, "Well, here goes. It starts over twenty years ago, when Mort Ramsey first comes to this country. He's all het up to make a million dollars. Gonna raise hell and put blocks under it. He's got a young, pretty wife, and they say he's out to prove he's good enough for her. He needs to show the world how well he did by marryin' her, and he needs to show her how far he can go. So he buys the ranch and does all right, but he doesn't cut the fat hog in the ass the way he wanted to, and he's afraid she'll leave him."

Ed shook his head. "Lot of trouble."

"That's just the start of it. He goes back to Nebraska, as the story goes, and he swindles a shit-pot full of money—from his own father, no less, and he takes her on a vacation back east. New York, Boston, Philadelphia, Washington, D.C. He pisses away the extra money, and they come home." Tyrel took a drink. "You know him, and you've met her, so you can imagine some of this."

Ed nodded as he put his pictures together.

"Well, he thought she was ungrateful, and she didn't like to be made to feel like she was bought and paid for, so she up and leaves him. By the way, we're gettin' into the part that you might not like."

"That's all right. I haven't liked some of it already."

"Good enough. So she leaves him. Now as the story goes, she has some help from another man. An older man, who was a foreman on a big cattle outfit north of Ashton, on the Cheyenne River. I think you can guess who I'm talkin' about."

"Jake Bishop."

"So then, as the story goes, she can't stay with him because she's trying to get a divorce. Hell of a mess, but she's got plenty on Ramses, includin' various ways he treated her physically, so she's got a case. She just has to stay away from this other man. Meanwhile he gets fired, so he goes down by the Rawhide Buttes and gets his own place to run a few cattle. Maybe she still sees him, but if she does, it's got to be on the sly because old Ramses has detectives out. Now somewhere in here a little baby comes along, a little boy, and the other man takes the kid to his place. The woman goes away, and the divorce case drags on. Are you sure you don't want a drink?"

"No, I'm fine."

"So after four or five years, this other man gets killed. People say that Ramses sent someone to do it, but no one can prove it, and to tell the truth, old Ramses had been so pious before about being the offended party, that there wasn't a real strong drive to find out who killed a man who took another man's wife. And at the time, this was still Laramie County, so the county seat and the sheriff were way the hell down in Cheyenne, and this was the middle of winter."

"I know. I remember the snow."

"When the law did come, they took the boy down to Cheyenne, and as I understand it, he was adopted out of there."

"By a family named Dawes."

"I would guess so." Tyrel paused to take a sip. "Now, how are we doin' on your questions?"

Ed felt as if he had a pound of cold iron in his stomach. "I've had a pretty strong suspicion all along that Mort Ramsey had him killed. Bridge had no personal reason, and Ramsey had all the motive in the world. Not the right, I don't think, but the motive."

"And your second question?"

"I'm not as worried as I was before that he might be my father, though even at that I had a pretty good idea that things were the way you tell them—about the three-sided thing, you know."

"I wasn't sure how you'd take it."

Ed shrugged. "The only parts that were brand-new were the details. As for the overall story, I was prepared for worse, about what any of the three might have done, or at what point the baby might have come along."

"Well, I've got to say, you took it on the chin."

"It wasn't that rough, and I appreciate you tellin' me what you know. Gettin' the story has been like tryin' to get water out of a stone."

"I'll tell ya. For the last few years, I've just been an old drunk, tryin' to laugh my way through the last part of life, but after what they did to Cam, I thought, if there's somethin' I can do to help someone catch up with these sons of bitches, then I'm satisfied." Tyrel gave a little frown. "What about the other questions?"

"There were one or two that would have come up if the answer to the second question had turned out different."

Tyrel looked at his drink. "I see. So they went away."

"Not entirely. I still remember them. But we can just say that I'm not done yet."

Chapter Fourteen

At the boarding house, Ed learned that Cam Shepard was still in something like a comatose state, as he did not talk or open his eyes. The doctor had left orders that he was not to be bothered, and the room was under lock and key.

Ravenna said she had a few minutes before she had to go to work on the evening meal, so she and Ed went out onto the back porch. They agreed that in broad daylight there wasn't much likelihood of an eavesdropper.

"This is a terrible thing that happened to Mr. Shepard," she began. "Mrs. Porter is outraged."

"She's got a right to be. I think it's a cowardly thing to do. On top of that, I feel guilty for it."

"Because he had been talking to you?"

"Yes. All it took was for the two riders I saw in the saloon to tell Ramsey I was talking to an old man of thus-and-such a description. Either that, or the bartender could have told him, or could have told someone else—Jeff, for example."

"Oh, him."

Ed quickened to her tone. "Has he been by again?"

"Once. The first night you were gone. He's so insistent, as if he thinks he has a claim, and his eyes—his looks are as bad as dirty words."

"He's dirty himself, listening in on other people's conversations, not to mention lookin' in through keyholes or windows. I was hopin' we wouldn't have any more to do with him, but it looks like I'll have to do something if I get through some of these other things all right. By the way, he knows Mr. Shepard, doesn't he?"

"Of course. He's met him several times."

"Did he talk to him the other night?"

"I don't think so, but I'm not sure."

"Well, I doubt that he would have gotten much out of him anyway. But he could have heard something in the saloon and passed it on, and Ramsey and his bodyguard took care of the rest."

Ravenna wore a pained expression. "But why would they do something so . . . so atrocious?"

Ed shifted his eyes and then met hers. "Well, to begin with, things were ready to blow open at the ranch. I hinted at that with you earlier."

She nodded.

"I didn't plan it at all. It just sort of happened, and I did what I had to do to get out of two different jams." He looked for her gesture to go on, and so he did. "First off, this fellow named Cooley, one of the regular men and a bully in his own right, wanted to push me around, rough me up, to find out why I was snoopin' for information about Mort Ramsey. Well—I didn't let him make mincemeat out of me. I left him in a gully, and as far as the rest of the ranch knew, he was missing."

"And you stayed there."

"Up till then, yes. Things were pretty tense, but no one knew anything for sure. Then the next day, this fella named Bridge—the one who killed Pa-Pa—got me off by myself and wanted to know what I knew about his pal disappearing. As far as I could tell, he didn't know I was on his trail or his boss's, or he would have shot me right there. But instead, he took me for a dummy, and I was able to get the drop on him. He wouldn't answer any questions, though, and when he tried to make a move on me, I had to let him have it."

Ravenna's eyes had a soft shine as they roved over him. "It sounds like either one of those situations could have been like poor Mr. Shepard's or worse. You came through it all right."

"I felt I was justified. Either of them would have finished me off with no conscience at all, and the second one had it coming from a long time ago, anyway."

"Oh, yes," she said.

"The way I see it, you can't just lie down and take it when they do something to someone close to you, much less when they want to do it to you."

Ravenna's hair waved as she moved her head from side to side. "Not at all. You were in the right."

"So then, as I told you before, I let on that I'd been fired, and I lammed out of there. That brought me to town, where I talked to Tyrel Flood and Cam Shepard, who sent me off to see someone else. This was in Ashton, a town that's on the other side of Glenrose."

"I see."

"He told me to go ask for a woman who used to be married to this Mort Ramsey."

"Oh. And did you find her?"

"Yes, I did. But she didn't want to talk about anything. So I left, and then she called me back—or her lawyer did."

"She changed her mind?"

"To begin with, it seemed like all the lawyer wanted to do was impress me with how much better it would be if I just dropped everything."

"Were they afraid of what he would do, or were they trying to protect him?"

"That's what I couldn't figure out, but I told him I was going to go ahead and do what I had to do anyway. That's when she agreed to talk to me again."

"This is interesting."

"I should say so. It turned out that all she wanted was to protect herself."

Ravenna's eyes widened. "You mean she had something to do with—"

"That's just it. She didn't understand what I was trying to get at, because they wouldn't let me come right out and ask my questions. They were thinkin' on another track. Before we were very long into this second conversation, she broke down and told me how sorry she was for leaving me to make my own way in the world."

"Ed!" she gasped. "Does that mean she was your—"

"Exactly. And I never guessed it, sitting there, while all the time she thought that was why I came."

"That must have been an incredible conversation. Did she ask you all about your life, how you grew up, what you're doing now?"

Ed shook his head. "That was the most curious part. It seemed as if once she had opened that box, she wanted to close it. As she phrased it to me, she just wanted to make her peace."

"To say she was sorry."

"Yes, and she did that. But she didn't try to be a mother to me at this late point."

Ravenna frowned. "You'd think she'd want to know more."

"You'd think so, but I believe she'd accepted long ago that she had given up being a mother. It seemed she just wanted to come out of it now without getting hurt. Once she had made her peace, as she said, she kept the conversation as short as possible. She didn't want complications."

"And you?"

"I could tell it was causing her a lot of turmoil, and I didn't want to see her cry. I told her it was all right, that growing up without a mother seemed normal to me—or the way life was, I think I put it. I told her I forgave her."

"You did? Why, Ed, that was a kind thing to do."

"I didn't think about it very much. The words just came out."

"And there wasn't much more to it than that? Than what you've told me, that is?"

"No, that's about it. Next thing I knew, I was back out on the street, and I didn't get a chance to ask her about Jake Bishop."

"Pa-Pa."

"Right."

"And furthermore, once I found out what she was to me, I had to consider whether this man she had been married to was my father."

"Oh, I hope not."

"And if so, what I could do about it."

Ravenna's eyes were opened wide. "But if he killed Pa-Pa, or had him killed—"

"I know. And the idea of having someone like that for a father is—"

"Repulsive."

"A good word. Meanwhile, the fellow comes to town and beats up an old drunk, or has it done."

Ravenna shook her head in slow motion.

Ed waited a few seconds to speak again. "When I got back here an hour or so ago, I went to see Tyrel Flood. He didn't want to give me much information before, but after what they did to Cam Shepard, and after I told him what I'd found out, he told me the fuller story."

"Was he afraid before?"

"I think so, and with good reason, when you see what happened to Cam. And besides, some people don't like to go diggin' up the past."

Ravenna's eyes had taken on a serious glint. "How would you feel about yourself if you didn't?"

"I know. You and I think the same on this. I couldn't have done otherwise." He patted her hand. "But anyway, back to what Tyrel told me."

"I'm sorry. Go ahead."

"That's all right." He kissed her quick, then paused for a few seconds and went on. "A long time ago—before I was born, at least—this fellow Mort Ramsey married a woman. I'll just call her Leah to make things easy. That's her name. He brings her out here, buys a ranch, wants to cut a better figure in the world, swindles a bunch of money from his own father, and she leaves him. It seems he mistreats her, too. Anyway, Jake Bishop helps her leave. He's a little older than she is, but not too old to have a romance with her." Ed paused. "That sounds like a soft word for all of this, but we'll leave it at that. So she goes into divorce proceedings, and meanwhile she has a baby, which ends up staying with Jake Bishop. She has to make herself scarce for purposes of the divorce, which she finally wins. But someone kills Jake Bishop. People assume it was someone sent by Mort Ramsey, but after all, the man took his wife, or something like it, though he didn't end up with her, so no one is urgent to look into it. The baby gets taken to Cheyenne and gets adopted out to a farm family."

"Then he's not your father."

"It doesn't seem like it."

"And yet your mother is so—I don't know. Cold isn't the word."

"No, I don't think it is. My belief is that through all of this, the best she's been able to do is try to save herself. At least she's done that, and I can tell it hasn't been easy on her."

"It hasn't been easy for you, either, and yet you have it in you to feel for her."

"That's a little strange in itself. It's not my usual way. When I was on the farm, for example, when one of the little Dawes kids would fall down or get hurt, I couldn't stand to hear the brat cry. Same as one day last year, out at the Tompkins Ranch. Little boy falls out of a tree he should never have been climbing and screams bloody murder, and I've got no feelin' at all for him. Same for old people. I just didn't want to know about someone else's pain or suffering. But when I was sitting in that lawyer's waiting room with a woman who was a complete stranger to me, and she started to cry, why, I felt for her."

"And you didn't have any sense that she was your mother?"

Ed shook his head. "None at all, at that moment."

"They say people can recognize those things naturally."

"Maybe some people can, but I didn't."

"Well, it was good of you to treat her well, before and after you knew what she was to you."

Ed shrugged. "It seemed like the only way to be. And as for her wanting to leave things as they are, that was acceptable. After all, how can you suddenly care about somebody you've never known—care about in that way, I mean."

Ravenna sighed. "I don't know. I guess you can't."

"It hasn't changed much, really. It hasn't changed who I am, or what I think I need to do."

Her eyes quickened. "Are you going to go to the ranch?"

"I think that's my next move. From the looks of things, Ramsey must be feeling pretty desperate right now, or he wouldn't have done what he did. My guess is that he came lookin' for me, and when he couldn't find me, he took it out on poor Cam. I suppose he hightailed it back to the ranch after that."

"There's been a lookout, but no one has seen either of them."

"I'd say that whether he knows who I am or not, he's found Bridge and Cooley by now, and he knows someone's on his trail. Feels driven into a corner."

"It sounds so dangerous, Ed."

"He's always been dangerous, or at least since I was born. It's just that he's on his guard against me now."

"And you're sure you're going out there?"

"I've got to. I can't rest until I do. I can't wait for him to come after me, get me in my sleep or when my back is turned." A thought crossed his mind. "By the way, there's something I want to show you."

She gave him a quizzical look.

"You still have that inventory, don't you?"

"Yes. Do you want me to get it?"

"I have something to add to it."

"All right. Give me a minute."

When she came back, she had the sheet of paper in one hand and an envelope in the other.

"This just came for you," she said, handing him the envelope as she sat down.

All it had on the outside was two lines of lettering printed by hand:

Edward Dawes

Litch, Wyoming

He set it aside and reached into his boot.

"I want to add this to the inventory," he said, setting the bone-handled sheath knife in its scabbard on the table.

She sat with the pencil poised. "What should I call it?"

"A hunting knife." He drew it out and showed the shiny, curved blade about five inches long. "Bone handle, curved blade, leather scabbard. I had it in my warbag before and didn't think of it."

He set the bare knife on the table, and as Ravenna wrote down the notations, his eyes lit on the letter he had set aside.

"Let's see what this is." He saw that it was an envelope with a letter inside, not just a piece of paper written on, folded up, and sealed. He picked up the knife and with very light pressure cut the folded edge of the envelope. Inside was a sheet of paper enclosing a smaller piece wrapped in tissue. He unfolded the letter and read it:

Edward:

It wasn't until after you left, and I thought about how surprised you seemed by the conversation, that I realized you may have come to ask about more than what we spoke of. Further, I admit that I was still protecting myself against what others might say or think.

So I send you this. It is the only one I have, or had, as it is now yours.

I thank you again for understanding.
L.C.

Ed began to unwrap the tissue. He could tell it was a photograph, about two inches by three. When he had it unwrapped, he turned it over, and a face looked back at him. It was a studio portrait of a man thirty-five or forty years old, before his hair turned grey. His hair was neatly combed, and he was clean-shaven. He wore a dark suit and vest with a white shirt and light-colored tie. From beneath dark brows, a pair of eyes looked at Ed—the eyes of a man who years ago had cared for him like a father.

"What is it?" said Ravenna, coming around to his side and looking on.

"Pa-Pa."

She took a few seconds to respond. "There's no question, is there?"

"No, none at all."

* * * * *

The buckskin stepped out at a brisk trot in the cool of morning. As Ed left the town of Litch behind him, he realized he could not take for granted that he would see the town again or any of the people in it. He brushed the thought from his mind and tried to think only of what lay ahead of him. Even at that, he did not have a definite plan because he did not know how things would take place. His idea was to confront Mort Ramsey, give him a chance to confess, and decide from there. It hadn't worked with Bridge, and Ed doubted that it would work with Ramsey, but he would give him a chance if the chips fell that way. As Ed saw it, a man deserved to have his say. Ed was not going to snipe and run in the style of a hired killer.

He came to the valley of dead cottonwoods in early afternoon. Once again the leafless trees looked spectral, and in their placement along the winding course of the creek bottom, they had the appearance of a procession of ancient skeletons.

Ed swung down from the horse and led it through the colony of abandoned prairie dogs to the waterhole. The afternoon was hot and dry as his boots moved through the brittle grass, but thunderclouds were forming along the hills far off to the west. It was the time of year for heavy thunderstorms, and he recalled the hailstorm he and the others at the Tompkins Ranch had seen the year before.

Keeping an eye on the clouds when he mounted up again, he rode through the broken country until the trail rose and came out in the broader terrain. The King Diamond Ranch was still a few miles off, and raindrops began to patter in the dust and raise the smell of rain coming to dry country.

As the drops started coming down heavier, Ed looked for a place to find shelter. He didn't care to have all of his gear wet, much less be pelted by hailstones, and he didn't want to ride into the ranch headquarters soaking wet like a muskrat.

Off to the west a couple of hundred yards, he saw where a gully rose up to a rocky overhang. It looked as if could get out of the worst of the shower there, but if the water began to come down in heavy sheets, he would have to look out for a flash flood. The clay on the underside of that rock looked as if it had been carried away by gully-washers.

He spurred the buckskin down into the gully, which was still only speckled damp and dry, and came up under the ledge of rock. A few drops sprayed in from the north, but for the most part, it was a good natural shelter. Ed dismounted and kept an eye out for snakes as the buckskin edged up closer to the dry wall.

The rain came down but not in torrents. It was settling the dust, washing off the sagebrush and cactus, soaking into the black roots of the buffalo grass. As far as Ed could see in any direction, which was a mile at the most because of his position, the wide land was taking in the moisture.

Movement caught his eye. Movement and shape, off to the east along the trail he had been riding. A man on a horse. Whoever it was, he hadn't been on the trail a minute earlier. He had come up from lower country to the east, had cut the trail, and now was headed north.

At first it looked like a figure in a cape, as if a rider of death had come up from the graveyard of cottonwoods, but then Ed saw that the man was wearing a dark slicker, wet now, and billowing out with the wind to make him look like a hunchback. The man's profile was hard to determine, and he wore no hat. He kept his face turned from the brunt of the wind-blown rain, and he did not seem to have the easy posture of a practiced rider of the range.

For a moment the wind slackened. The slicker lost its billow, and the rider faced the trail ahead of him. As Ed identified the hatless burr head, he realized it was the first time he had seen George the brute on horseback. Ed breathed a long sigh, as quiet as he could make it. This little hideout was a good place to be—much better than having the brute in the dark slicker coming up the trail behind him.

Chapter Fifteen

All the way in on the trail from the main road to the ranch headquarters, Ed kept an eye on the tracks ahead of him. The rain had penetrated the loose dirt about half an inch and the hard earth quite a bit less, so it was easy to see where each step of the horse had cut through the damp to the dry.

When the trail turned and went south down the open slope to the ranch buildings, the tracks did not waver. As Ed came to the bunkhouse, he saw that the rider had taken the horse straight on down to the barn.

One thing at a time, Ed thought. Unless Pat the cook had been ordered to shoot him on sight, Ed could ask a couple of questions and try to find out how things stood. But he was sure of one thing, after having seen George out on the trail. They were expecting him here at the King Diamond. With his stomach tightening, he swung down at the hitching rail and tied his horse. He crossed the bare dirt, paused on the stone doorstep, and opened the door.

"Anybody home?" he called out. As the door swung the rest of the way open and his vision came around, he saw a man sitting at the table, facing the door as Bridge had done. But it was not Bridge. It was someone thicker in build, but not as big as Cooley. Ed recognized the form and then the sarcastic voice.

"Well, look who comes in the door. It's our little two-fisted Romeo."

"I didn't expect to see you here, Jeff."

"Land of many surprises. Where did you expect to see me—in Ashton?"

"Now that I think of it, this is the most likely place. Mindin' the main chance, aren't you?"

"What's wrong with that?"

"Probably nothing—for you."

Jeff stood up and looked over his shoulder at the cook, who stood slouching by the stove and smoking a cigarette. "Pat," he said, "this is the guttersnipe I told you about."

"I know."

Jeff stepped into the open, away from the end of the table. He was not wearing a hat or a gunbelt. "Come here, boy. Stand right here." He pointed at the space about an arm's length in front of him.

"What for?"

"So I can give you a lesson. Did you bring the boxing gloves?"

Ed swallowed hard. "I didn't think to."

"Stand over here, then. Don't be afraid." Jeff flicked his eyebrows in a smirk.

Ed slid a glance at Pat, who was looking at the end of his cigarette. He brought his eyes back to Jeff and took three steps forward and to his left. Turning square to face him, Ed raised his chin. "Go ahead. Throw the first punch."

Jeff smiled. "Not me. Not here." He rocked back onto his heels and forward again. "Now look here, boy. You don't tell me. I tell you. And when I tell you to do something, you do it."

"Why should I?"

"Didn't that little girl tell you? I'm the foreman here now."

Ed felt his head begin to swim, and he shook away the sensation. "You can leave her out of it. And as for you bein' foreman, I didn't come back here to take orders."

"Leave her out of it. I wouldn't do that for the world. When a fella's got a good thing, he wants his friends to be happy for him."

The pressure was rising. "I don't like the way you talk."

"That's because you don't understand. You're just a boy."

"What do you mean by that?"

"She knows what a man is."

Ed felt his chest rising, his fists doubling. He didn't have an answer.

"She knows all about it. The farmer in Crete taught her, but I taught her better."

"You're just a dirty peeping—"

"Easy, boy. Get used to it. She's going to have my baby."

A blood rage broke loose. Ed threw himself at Jeff, swinging, but the stocky man was waiting for him and caught him with a punch that knocked his hat off. Ed felt the blow, sharp and heavy on his temple, but it seemed distant in his blind fury. He kept swinging until he closed in on the man, and then he grabbed him and threw him to the floor. Jeff came up with both fists ready, his head lowered, and a menacing look on his face that reminded Ed that in Arkansas they fought for real.

Jeff came on with a rush, battering Ed's head and forearms with a series of right and left punches. Ed fell backwards, toward the open doorway, and Jeff piled on. Holding Ed's shirt front with one hand, he punched with the other. Then he shifted his left hand, grabbed Ed by the hair, and dug his thumb into Ed's eye socket.

Ed erupted with a primal burst of strength. He threw Jeff to one side, rose from the threshold, picked up the heavier man in a bear hug, and slammed him to the floor. He picked him up again, and Jeff twisted away, spilling out through the doorway and rolling in the dirt. Ed jumped after him, picked him up a third time, and slammed him for all he was worth. He straddled Jeff and sat on him, pinning the man with his weight on the man's abdomen and both hands on his throat.

"Take it back!" he commanded, his throat dry and harsh.

Jeff blew a puff of air and a small spray of spit.

"I said take it back!"

"Puh-puh-puh . . ."

Ed thought the man was going to finish the word, but instead he spit at Ed's face and bucked with his hips, as if he expected to throw Ed off. But Ed hung on. He tightened his grip on the man's throat and slammed his head on the stone doorstep half a dozen times, until the body went limp beneath his hands.

Ed pushed back and sat on his heels. He did not look straight at Jeff, but from his sideways glance, he saw the still body of a man who would rather fight to the finish than take back an empty taunt. It was too bad, but he asked for it.

Ed pushed himself to his feet, straightened up, and looked around. Just inside the doorway, Pat the cook was smoking his cigarette down to the pinched end.

"He was goin' to kill you."

Ed spoke between heaving breaths. "Well, he didn't get to." Ed gave another quick once-around. "Where's everyone else?"

Pat motioned with his hand toward Jeff's lifeless body. "He put' em all to pilin' hay. I think he wanted 'em out of the way for this."

"It's just as well." Ed was sure now that they had been expecting him all along. He pulled in a deep breath and tried to settle himself down. His hands were shaking, and his knees felt as if they were going to give out. "Is Ramsey in the big house?"

"I don't know. You'll have to go see."

That was Pat—wait to see who came out on top.

Ed stepped inside the bunkhouse and found his hat. After putting it on, he checked to see that the sheath knife was still on his belt, halfway around from his pistol. Having gotten most of his wind back, he went out into the sunlight and turned to go to the ranch house.

Nothing moved in the yard. Ed wondered if George the brute had finished with the horse and had come to the house, but he did not see any footprints or turned earth to suggest it. The man could have come the back way, of course.

Ed raised his eyes and glanced around. With the storm having passed over, the afternoon had cleared. The sun was bright, and the air was fresh. At times like this, after a summer storm, it was common to hear meadowlarks, but at the moment, no sounds came on the clear air. Nor did any sounds come from the corrals or barn—no hooves thumping on rails or posts, no horses nickering. A dead silence hung over the whole yard, as if the gables and dormers of the lodge-like house had frowned everything into muteness.

As Ed went up the heavy plank steps to the porch, he saw that the door was ajar. Drawing his pistol, he nudged the door with the toe of his boot. A faint jingle made him wish he had taken off his spurs. The door moved without a noise from the hinges. There came only the sound, or the movement of air that seemed like sound, of the heavy wooden object swinging inward.

He drew his gun and took a step inside, then another, sending the faint ring of a spur with each step. The door to the office area ahead was open, but the room was not lit, and the partial view of the desk did not show anyone sitting there. Maybe the master was waiting in another room or in a dark corner of this one. Maybe the brute was still in the barn and had not come in the back way. Maybe they were both in the cellar.

Ed took another step, trying to set his foot down softly so as not to make a sound with the spur. Now another step. His eyes were adjusting to the dark interior, and he could make out the open beams of the vaulted ceiling.

Wham! A rushing force hit him sideways on the right, knocking the gun from his hand and sending it in a thumping rattle across the floor. He felt his arm pinned to his side as a demonic shriek pierced his ear. He smelled the rank odor of man-sweat, and he felt the chin of the brute dig into his shoulder as he was lifted from the floor.

He kicked, he squirmed, he swung with his left fist. The brute shook him and tightened the hug. Ed swung again, and his fist glanced off the side of the brute's sweaty head.

"Hold still," came Ramsey's voice, "or I'll stick this gun in your mouth and pull the trigger." When the struggling subsided, the click of a pistol hammer sounded, as if Ramsey had been waiting for the moment to make his emphasis.

Ed could not find the floor with his feet. The locked grasp of George the brute held him up like a sack of grain or a quarter of beef.

"We'll take him to the bridal chamber, George. But before we go, let me tell you this, young snoop. You do what you're told." His tone of voice changed as he said, "Just hold him for a minute, George." Then he addressed Ed again in his commanding tone. "Like I was saying, you do what you're told. You'll see why we call it the bridal chamber. When you put a gun to a man's head, he'll do anything to keep you from pulling the trigger. Anything. So just do what you're told. Let's go, George."

The brute relaxed his grip in order to heft the burden and get a new purchase on it, and when he did, Ed exploded. With a burst of power, he kicked and twisted, then pounded George square on the cheekbone. He hooked a boot behind the brute's knee, and with that as his base, he pushed with his whole body, driving his right shoulder at George's chest.

The brute staggered and took a step backwards. Ed twisted again, punched him in the face, then wedged his left arm between them and shoved. The brute toppled and hit the floor, and Ed broke free from the tangle.

George was back on his feet right away, grabbing at Ed and blocking off any chance Ramsey might have had to pull the trigger. This time the brute grabbed Ed's left forearm and settled on it with the iron grip of his right hand. Ed twisted his arm down, around, and up, breaking the grip but allowing George to close in on him. The brute was bringing his right arm up and around, skidding off Ed's shoulder and hooking around his neck.

Ed's left arm had slipped in back of the brute's waist, while his right hand had fumbled for the sheath knife. He could feel the bone handle in his grip. George's arm was closing around his neck now, the sweaty wrist like a vise, bringing Ed's face against the brute's chest. Ed drew his hips back to give himself room, but he hung onto George's waist to stay aligned, and then with an upward thrust, he drove the knife blade into the brute's mid-section.

The hammerlock relaxed, and a more inhuman cry than before filled the vaulted room. The brute dropped to his knees, then slumped over to his side on the floor.

Ed searched in the dusky shadows, expecting a bullet any second, but instead he heard a scramble and saw a human form go through the office doorway. The light closed off, and the door slammed. Ed put his hands on his knees and bent over, pulling in air and trying to catch his breath all over again.

Some light was coming in through the front door—not enough to reach into the darker recesses but enough to let Ed see that George the brute was finished. Ed walked to the body, leaned over, wiped the blade of his knife on the dead man's shirt, and put the knife in its sheath. Standing up, he looked around for his gun. His head was moving up and down as he continued pulling in deep gulps of air. Finding the gun where it had fallen, he picked it up and put in his holster.

Now it was time for quiet movement again. Ed thought of taking off the spurs, but they were too bulky and sharp to stow in a pocket, and he didn't want to leave them behind in case he had to leave this place in a hurry. So he kept them on and tried to take soft steps.

He paused at the door to the office, tried to quiet his breathing, and listened. No sounds came. He pictured Ramsey seated behind the desk and pointing a pistol at the door—or maybe a shotgun from the glass-and-wood case behind the desk, as he recalled. He tried the knob. It turned, but the door was locked. He expected a bullet to come ripping through the door panel, but silence hung on. He rattled the door knob, then listened. Still no sound. He wondered if Ramsey went out the window. It would be an effort for the heavy man, and a bit of a drop to the ground, but he could do it.

Ed rattled the door knob again, and when he had scarcely let it go, he leaned back and kicked the knob square with the sole of his boot.

The door flew open, splintering the door jamb, and from where he had jumped to one side, Ed could see there was no one in the room. Stepping inside, he saw that the window was latched. That could not have been done by anyone crawling out.

The gun case. Ed went to it and inspected around its edges, looking for a hinge or crack but finding none. The case was built into the wall and varnished all the way around. He stood back and surveyed the wall. Above the gun case, a set of deer antlers was mounted on a varnished wood plaque, which in turn was attached to the wall with two brass screws with large round heads. The wall was a solid piece.

Turning to the left side of the room, which had a ceiling-high bookcase running its length, he continued his search. He knew the bookcase didn't lead to anything, because on the other side of this wall was an open room, a continuation of the front room with the high ceiling.

Ed looked up at the low ceiling of the office. He saw that it had no hatchway, so he went back to examining the bookcase. At last he found a latch, inside the right end of the middle shelf. It was a rounded brass plate with indentations for his fingertips. Pressing the heel of his hand against the trim of the bookcase, he squeezed the latch toward him and heard a click.

The wall with the gun case moved a quarter of an inch away, and Ed gave it a push. It swung into dark empty space, where the musty smell of a cellar rose up and a set of wooden steps led down into darkness. Ramsey was hidden in there somewhere, and Ed had to go down and get him.

Leaving the hinged wall open to give him whatever light straggled in, Ed went down the stairs, troubled at each step by the sound of a spurred boot. At the bottom, he moved into darkness. He had no idea what the layout was like, and he didn't dare light a match and make himself a target.

If all Ramsey wanted to do was hide, he could do that well enough. But he couldn't shoot at his pursuer down in this hole, not without light, and he would have a hard time going past him to get back upstairs. Once the pursuer knew about it, this hole wasn't much good for a man alone. It didn't make enough sense.

Of course. No one with Ramsey's devious mind would have a hole with only one way out. The trouble was, he knew where the other exit was and could find it in the dark. The pursuer couldn't. Ed imagined that Ramsey had come up like a gopher somewhere and was coming around the front way to get the drop on Ed when he came out of the office or up out of the cellar.

Now was a time to do something about the jingling noise. Holstering his gun, Ed sat down in the dark and pulled off his boots. Next he unbuckled each spur and tucked it into its respective boot. Then, holding the pair by the pull straps, he drew his gun and walked back to the faint light coming down the staircase.

Ramsey could be waiting for him in the office, but Ed had to take that chance. The big boss could even close the passage and have Pat stand guard with a shotgun until the other men came in. Ed couldn't wait and let him do something like that, either.

Sock-footed, he went up the steps, keeping to his left so that the boards wouldn't creak and so that he wouldn't make as good a target. He ducked under the dummy wall where it hung out over the chasm, and he moved on up into the office. Still nothing.

He crossed the office and paused at the doorway, then stepped through and to one side in order not to make a silhouette. Searching the dusky room, he saw a shape that gave him a start. Ramsey was kneeling by the dead body of George the brute and was hovering over it. Ed imagined the man was checking for signs of life and in his focused attention had not heard any padded footsteps. Yet the two shadowy forms looked like something other than human—like two ungainly creatures, one giant turtle trying to climb over another.

Ed held his boots out to his side at arm's length and dropped them. As Ramsey rose up with a jerk, Ed said, "Careful, Mort. Take it slow. I'm the one with the gun now." He clicked the hammer to make his point.

Ramsey stood up. "I know who you are."

"You know a lot."

"You're the bastard."

The word stung, but Ed held the gun firm. "And you're the killer. Not man enough to do it yourself, but brave enough to hire it done."

"And you've been to see the whore."

"Don't worry about her."

"Never happy unless she could have another man." Ramsey's form wavered in the shadowy light that faded where he stood.

"Hold still."

"So you're giving orders. Who do you think you are? A little pup that should have been drowned before it opened its eyes."

"Well, they've been opened." Ed glanced at the dead form and back at Ramsey. "As for who I think I am, I'll tell you what I told Bridge. I told him it was my turn to be the stranger who came to call. That's where we are now. I gave him a chance to have his say, and I'm givin' you the same."

"To have my say about what?"

"About Jake Bishop."

Ramsey was silent for a couple of seconds. Then he spoke as he took a step to his right. "A little slobbering blind pup with its tongue stuck out where it was pulled from its mother's tit."

"Keep still."

Ramsey took another step to get around the body on the floor. "Wet behind the ears. Did you come here wet from her bed as well?"

Ed's hand was shaking, and he felt like shouting, but he said in a calm voice, "I told you to hold still."

"I piss on you and your—" Ramsey pulled at the ivory-handled gun and had it halfway up when Ed pulled the trigger.

The big man flinched with the shock. He straightened up and held his arms close in to his chest with his hands flared outward, so that in silhouette he looked like a toad on its back. Then he fell slumped over the body of his henchman.

* * * * *

It did not take long for Ed to put on his boots, find a couple of kerosene lamps, and get a fire going. With Pat looking on, Ed waited outside until flames broke through the roof. With black smoke billowing for the men to see from the hayfield, he mounted the buckskin and rode away from the King Diamond Ranch in Thunder Basin.

* * * * *

After a camp in the open, Ed arrived at the Iris at mid-morning. Ravenna met him in the dining room and told him right away that Cam Shepard had died the day before.

"It's too bad," she said, leading the way to the back porch. "Even if his health was not good, he could have lived a little longer."

Outside, in the shade of the porch, Ed looked around to make sure no one was nearby. "Well, the ones who did it can't answer for any more than they already have."

She turned to let her eyes meet his. "Then you—"

"Yes, I did. They would have gotten me if I hadn't. They were looking for me already. And by the way, it did seem as if they forced something out of Cam Shepard, for all the good it did them."

Her eyes seemed to be taking in all of him in a positive appraisal. "I'm glad you came out of it all right."

"So am I, of course. It helped to know that you were behind me. You believed in me."

"And I still do." Standing next to him, she joined her hand with his.

"I appreciate it. You know, through all of this, it's seemed that you and I have a lot in common. We grew up outside the regular pattern of things, and we've had to take life as it was handed to us."

Her eyes were at once hard and soft as they met his again. "And we both believe that people shouldn't get away with things that aren't right."

He took her in his arms for a long kiss. Releasing, he said, "I was afraid to do too much of this before I got those other things settled. I was afraid the thoughts would distract me, get me off track."

"Now you can do it as much as you want." She gave him back all his kiss, and more.

"Whew!" he said, straightening his hat and catching his breath. "We need to go away somewhere."

Her eyes were sparkling. "You think so?"

"Yes, but before we do anything else, I want to show you something."

"Not the bone-handled—"

"No. Something round and a little more feminine." He drew from his pocket the small pasteboard box.

A smile played on her face as she took the package, opened it, and unwrapped the little bundle in tissue. She placed the ring in her bare palm, where the deep red gem sparkled. "It's beautiful."

"The jeweler said it's a garnet. I hope you can accept it from Mr. Edward Bishop."

She kissed him again, light and lovely. "I don't see why not."

About the Author

John D. Nesbitt is the author of more than forty books, including traditional westerns, crossover western mysteries, contemporary western fiction, retro/noir fiction, nonfiction, and poetry. He has won the Western Writers of America Spur Award four times—twice for paperback novel, once for short story, and once for poem. He has won the Western Fictioneers Peacemaker Award twice—once for novel and once for short story. He has been a finalist for the Spur Award twice, the Peacemaker seven times, and the Will Rogers Medallion Award eight times. He has also received two creative writing fellowships with the Wyoming Arts Council—once for fiction, once for nonfiction—and he has won the fiction award four times with the Wyoming State Historical Society. He lives in the plains country of Wyoming, where he is Professor Emeritus of English and Spanish at Eastern Wyoming College. Visit his website at www.johndnesbitt.com

Now Available!

SPUR AWARD-WINNING AUTHOR
JOHN D. NESBITT

Action / Adventure Westerns

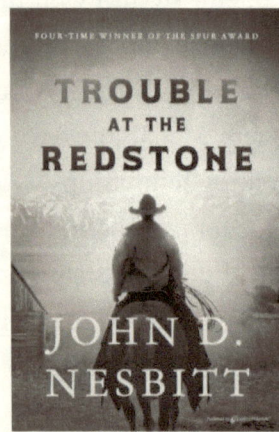 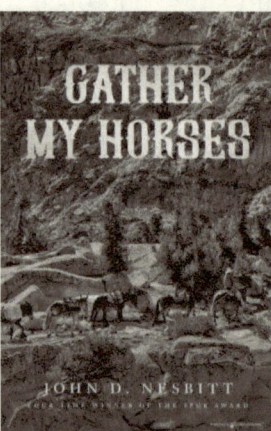 

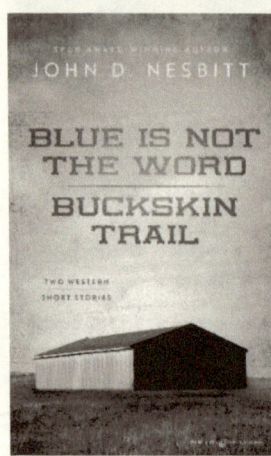  

**For more information
visit: SpeakingVolumes.us**

Now Available!

FROM MASTER STORYTELLER
DAN JORGENSEN

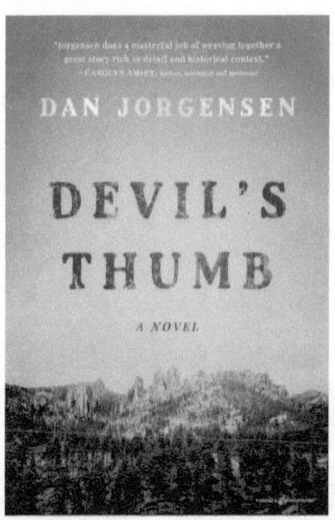

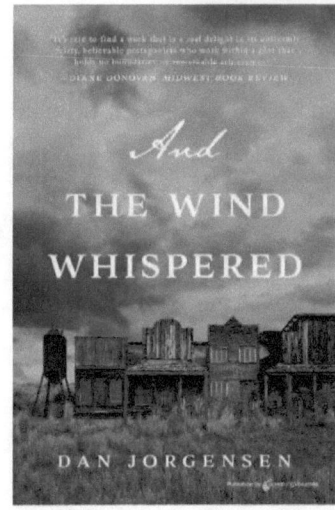

For more information
visit: SpeakingVolumes.us

Now Available!

SPUR AWARD-WINNING AUTHOR
ROD MILLER

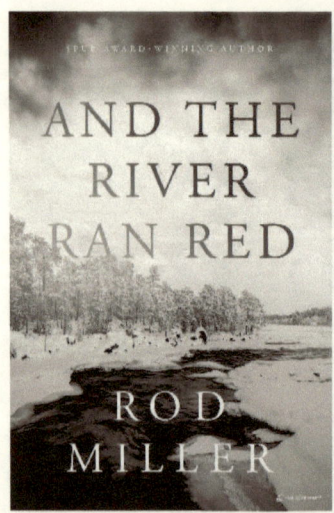

**For more information
visit: SpeakingVolumes.us**

www.ingramcontent.com/pod-product-compliance
Lightning Source LLC
LaVergne TN
LVHW041702070526
838199LV00045B/1167

TO&E   Table of Organization and Equipment. The list of personnel and equipment needed and authorized for each unit.

TOC   Tactical Operations Center

VC   Vietcong. The revolutionary soldiers of the indigenous population.

Vulcan Cannon   A 7.62MM automatic gun with a series of rotating barrels that fires two to three thousand rounds per minute.

www.ingramcontent.com/pod-product-compliance
Lightning Source LLC
LaVergne TN
LVHW041701070526
838199LV00045B/1149